EMPTY SADDLES

Corral de Terra Ranch—the battlefield of an ancient feud between cattlemen and sheepmen. Its bullet-riddled walls told their story of half-forgotten gunfights. They flung a silent challenge to Dare Devlyn, and he decided to buy the place and reap its exciting heritage.

But the feud had been buried thirty years ago—when the last of the Jessimer brothers had fled the country. And Dare believed he was cheated of the excitement he sought.

Yet old-time ranchers warned him to go slow with his dealings with the sheepmen—that under the surface the feud still smoldered.

Unwittingly, Dare fanned it into flame...

EMPTY SADDLES

Cherry Wilson

This hardback edition 2001
by Chivers Press
by arrangement with
Golden West Literary Agency

ISBN 0 7540 8127 3

British Library Cataloguing in Publication Data available

Printed and bound in Great Britain by
Redwood Books, Trowbridge, Wiltshire

CONTENTS

CONTENTS

EMPTY SADDLES

CHAPTER I

CORRAL DE TERRA

TOWARD the end of a perfect day in June,
Dare Devlyn galloped into the Los Lobos Range.
Free as the prairie wind that blew, without a care
for the future, a regret for the past, or a tie to bind.
With ten thousand dollars burning a hole in his
pocket! On a fast paint pony that was the living response to a cowboy's prayer, and with the flashiest,
classiest outfit money could buy. His bridle and
breast collar were lavishly mounted with silver, and
his heavy, hand-tooled, Garcia saddle was most ex-
quisitely silver wrought—even to the tapaderos, so
sweeping that the tips brushed the earth in his gallop, raising twin streamers of dust.

Nor was Dare exactly a blot on the landscape himself. A costly black beaver sombrero shaded his
darkly handsome, reckless, young face. His shirt,
rippling and swelling as he rode, was of purest silk
and a turquoise hue; silken, too, the black bandanna
that jauntily fluttered about his throat. His slim
waist was cinched with a wide belt that was not
merely a belt—but a masterpiece of the silversmith's
art. And, like unto the stars on the Milky Way,
silver conchas sprinkled the wide wings of his leather
chaps.

Just the same, Dare's dark eyes were cloudy with strange discontent. Strange—because he had, right in sight, everything any cowboy could want. Everything *he* had wanted at the time luck played him for a favorite, handing him a legacy of twelve thousand dollars, when he was just a forty-a-month waddy on a Pecos River ranch. But after he had bought everything—Check, the fast, flashy paint stepping under him now, this bang-up new outfit and all—he had a sudden craving for something that was not for sale. An irrational, irrepressible hunger for adventure—red-hot and sizzling, right off the smoking griddle of life. And, sure that adventure haunted strange trails —since he had never met any at home—Dare had set out to find it.

Many highly exciting things are apt to happen to a quixotic and devil-may-care young buckaroo with ten thousand dollars. So it is little short of a miracle that—in the six weeks since he had quit the Pecos in a blaze of glory, glittered through the Apache country, dazzled the Rio Grande, and left the Alamosa Range to blink at his passing—not a single thing had happened. Nothing, at least, that could not have happened at home. And now Dare was in the Los Lobos Range, despairing of anything ever happening again.

Always the Los Lobos had meant adventure to him. Why, the whole Southwest had still been heated up over the terrible range war here when he was a kid! And he had heard so much of the exciting times it had been through that he had always been crazy to see it—thinking it would be like that yet. And now here he was; and it was—*dead!* This whole country—clear in from the Sulphur

Desert to the black ramparts of the Nimbres Mountains just ahead—was absolutely the deadest he had been through yet.

And the range underfoot was little more than a heap of dust, with nothing growing on it but mesquite and sage. The grass had been eaten down to the roots, and the roots cut out by hordes of sheep, whose tracks were the only sign of them left. "Sheeped out!" Dare's face expressed his supreme disgust.

Funny about that—he had always understood that the Los Lobos was straight cow range. Well, it was sure ruined now for either mutton or beef. A dead range! And all he wanted was to get out of it and go on—where? He had not any idea. He had been so sure of meeting real, live adventure here, that he had made no plans. Not much use going farther. Because, as he irritably confided to Check, "Everything worth happenin' had already happened before I was born!"

But he would not be caught dead on a sheep range. So, swinging Check toward the great sentinel peak that commanded every ridge, dome, and spire in the wild Nimbres—El Capitan, they had called it back at Red Dune, when they pointed the landmark out to him—Dare decided to make tracks for Sundown, spend the night there, and figure where next.

Galloping across country at a pace that made all his silverware jingle and flash, he was surprised to see that, in the very first mile, the range underwent a radical change for the better. There was grass here, and cattle. Puzzled to account for such a sharp contrast, he pulled up on a prairie rise and looked back.

Behind, below him, east, and west, as far as the eye could follow, ran a well-defined line. And south of it were the desolate, sheeped-out flats he had forsaken. North of it, the same land, the same soil, but with what a difference! For it was carpeted deep with mesquite grass—was rich, growing, *living*. And Dare guessed the reason. Some past controversy—doubtless the old range wars of which he had heard—had set that invisible line beyond which sheep could not pass. Well, it was not invisible now. And this side, the cattle side, was more what he had thought the Los Lobos would be like. A man's land! A real cow range. But he had to admit it was no more exciting.

And, as irksomely peaceful miles succeeded each other, he took out his discontent on the fence he was following. It was down most of the way, with every other post rotted out, and the wire treacherously snaked in the grass, a menace to range stock. Sulphurously, the cowboy expressed his opinion of a rancher who would let a fence lie like that. And he drew a vivid mind picture of just what that hombre's place would be like, to judge by the fence.

Then, loping with it around a low butte, just as the sun slid behind the grim battlements of El Capitan, he got the surprise of his life at sight of the ranch.

For the house—the grandest ranch home he had seen on his trip—was a huge adobe, such as could only belong to some cattle baron of the free-grass plains. It was set picturesquely at the foot of El Capitan, in a grove of giant black sycamores, with house, trees, and buildings inclosed by a high adobe wall. Wondering how such a place could be related to the wreck of a fence that ran right down and claimed it, he saw with surprise, as he neared, that the house was more or less of a wreck itself. It was deserted, and had been so for years. The doors were conspicuous by their absence. The windows could not boast a whole pane of glass. And weeds had taken possession of the place.

Mystified that a ranch like this should be deserted in the heart of a prosperous cattle range, Dare reined in beside the tumble-down gate. There, still, in the weathered crosspiece above, the name, Corral de Terra, was faintly traced.

Below, another sun-blistered legend crazily swung, announcing

For sale. See agent, Kit Kress, Sundown, N. M.

But Dare's eyes merely flicked over it and up again to the name of the ranch.

Corral de Terra! It beat like a pulse in his brain. He had heard of it. Where? He could not remember. But in a way that thrilled and chilled him just making the effort. Sitting there in the saddle, his brows puckered with the strain of remembering, his dark gaze on the house, he said it aloud—"Corral de Terra." And suddenly another name flashed into his mind—Jessimer! And the two put together made the sum total—danger! Why? He could not remember that either. But he knew they were mixed up with the black tales he had heard of the Los Lobos Range. And he decided to give the place the once-over before riding on.

As he pulled Check through the gate in the walled inclosure and rode up the overgrown drive, all at once a queer and shivery feeling came over him. Even the breeze—a balmy June breeze—blew in here with a strange chill, seemed to set the trees, vines, and weeds to whispering secrets—things too awful to tell. And he thought it must be the way the dead eyes of the old house stared out at him that made him feel so, or the utter desolation on every hand. But, looking back after, with the fearful wisdom of all that befell him, he knew it was the chill shadow of coming events. For—though he was unaware of it yet—his riding within the somber walls of Corral de Terra plunged him into the adventure he sought.

Leaving Check to crop the rank grass in the court, he passed by the house—for some reason he was never able to fathom—and set out to explore the buildings in the back. There was no slightest trace of a path. And his nerves tightened a notch as at every step weeds tangled in his spurs, almost tripping him up.

He found the corrals sagged, or fallen completely, the roof of the great barn caved in, and the walls leaning wearily on each other, in imminent danger of total collapse. A long shed, adjoining the barn, proved to be a mausoleum for the bones of a buckboard that was so ancient it threatened to crumble to dust at his touch. Skirting other vine-covered ruins that had been other sheds, he came to the bunk house—a wreck without and a litter within.

Going in, Dare's spirits hit bed rock. Here men like himself had lived and worked, as a thousand things told him—scraps of old leather, cinch rings and buckles, moldering, rat-eaten, worn old saddles. And the saddles spoke to him, as with living tongue, of the life and work of the boys who had gone. Empty saddles! They made him blue. Where were the boys who had ridden for Corral de Terra? Why had they left their saddles behind? Were they dead, too, like this place?

His sober gaze strayed to an old envelope that one of the saddles had lain upon and shielded from exposure these—thirty years, for he could make out the date. Thirty years! Eight more than he had lived. Through all of them, through all the years he had been on earth, this ranch had been abandoned like this!

Abruptly, he stepped outside again. A red-tailed hawk screamed in a sycamore, and Dare all but jumped out of his skin. Then, grinning at how he had let a deserted old ranch get on his nerves, he turned toward the house. Long, long ago, it had sprung from the red earth on which it stood, and was ever so slowly returning to dust. A wide gallery ran completely around it, settled and stooped as though weary of running. And here Dare halted to look about.

Sunset fired the beetling crags, towering over two thousand feet sheer. Its afterglow was red on the plains beyond. But Corral de Terra lay in the mountain's shade. Yet the shade was not so deep but that the court was a riot of color still—the glory of wild sunflower, the lilac of loco, all lupine blued, and with the tiny petals of shepherd's clock dotting the whole like scarlet rain.

Columbine flirted golden tassels from the grim old wall. A bird sang in the sycamores. But they were like flowers that nod over a grave, or a bird on a tombstone singing; for all the endeavor of flower and bird, the feeling of death was there, and a seeming stillness that deepened the nameless chill in the cowboy's veins.

And when he actually set foot on the gallery, something stopped him again. With head thrown back, he looked up through a rift in the trees at El Capitan—reared like a titanic monument over Corral de Terra's grave. Strangely, he wondered if it was something El Capitan had seen down here that had put that frozen look on its grim, old face. And he gazed, almost hopefully, down over the plains he had crossed for some sight of a ranch. But there was none to be seen in that fifty-mile scope. Those he had passed were hidden by buttes, or buried in the prairie swells.

And he complained: "It's so blamed God-forsaken. Like there wasn't a soul in the world but me!" Yet more fantastically he went on: "It's like the castle in that fool fairy tale that lay for a hundred years in a spell, till the weeds growed up in a forest, an' a hombre come along an' kissed the princess sleepin' in it. It's like Corral de Terra's laid in a spell, waitin' for me——" He blushed, as his mind completed the simile, at the mere thought of being required to kiss even a hundred-year-old princess.

Shrugging such fancies from him, he crossed the gallery. And, with nerves mysteriously taut, heart beating hard, he was in the doorway, when——

"How do you do?"

A cool, sweet, *princessy* voice from out the musty old house froze Dare on the threshold.

He tried to get his tongue down from the roof of his mouth to where he could use it, since he knew it was not polite for a puncher to keep any kind of a princess waiting.

"Oh!" exclaimed the haughty voice, as though that settled it all. "So you brought out my dress—the little red velvet!"

Still dumb with the shock of that, Dare saw her —the princess! Not sleeping, of course, but arrayed in a purple robe and a diadem, doing her stuff. And she was so lovely—with her face set like a little pale moon in the dead night of her hair; and so graceful and dignified, in that purple robe that hung from her shoulders and swept out in a train—that he would have been tongue-tied with awe, if he *had* been her lackey and brought out her dress. But now he saw that she was not talking to him at all. Instead, she was greeting some one whom he could not see, in that door on the opposite side of the hall.

"Really, Mrs. Hutchins," said the slim little princess —in a tone Dare thought royalty reserved for "Off with his head!"—"you shouldn't have gone to all that trouble. You know I send away for all my creations. This little red velvet—well, I simply had to have some kind of a rag for garden wear."

Still, though Dare's eyes fairly leaped from his head, he could not catch a ghost of a glimpse of the person she talked to.

"Please," she sweetly reproved the thin air, "after this, deliver *all* goods in the rear. I don't know what my visitors would think to see a *trades person* come to the front! But I'll overlook it this once. You've had a hot ride? Well, Mrs. Hutchins, you'd better come in and rest a bit."

Then goose flesh stood out all over Dare, and cold

chills played fox-and-geese the full length of his spine. For, still graciously conversing in that bright, cold, little voice that made him think of a blade in a sheath, *she ushered nobody in!* And she walked and talked with nobody halfway down the hall! Telling nobody how her guests were out amusing themselves, and she'd given the servants the afternoon off, and it was so nice to have a little time to herself!

Spellbound with horror, Dare saw her seat nobody in a decrepit old chair before the dead fireplace, sweep regally out, and come back like a queen, with an imaginary goblet, and give nobody a drink! And just when he was within an ace of shaking completely out of his boots, she began to speak to her imaginary visitor.

"Old friends?" Her brows protestingly arched to a remark nobody had made. "But really, Mrs. Hutchins, how can that be? Why, I'm not even an old *customer!* You say you met me ages ago? You knew me when—— No, I'm sorry, I don't remember." And without the slightest warning, she shot out a royal little foot, upset the chair, and, quivering over the nonexistent, but supposedly prostrate Mrs. Hutchins, cried like a regular human

"Yes, you old hellion—*you bet I do!*"

The tension on Dare's nerves snapped, and he broke into a loud, hysterical laugh. The girl whirled, chalk-white, her great eyes dilated with fright. Her hands, flying in fear to her throat, released the robe and it fell to the floor, revealing that which sent the cowboy into another convulsion of mirth. And the happy tears of it filled his eyes, so he did not see the little figure stiffen in agony, or the burning blood of mortification whip flame to her cheeks. But, with such pain as he had never heard, her cry cut to him:

"Laugh!" The voice instantly killed all desire to laugh within him. "Go on—laugh! It's funny, ain't it? *Me*—tryin' to be a lady! *Me*—makin' out like I am somebody! But it's on you, stranger, for—I—ain't—worth—laughin' at!"

Her voice had choked, and Dare had the horrible fear that she was going to cry, when pride came to her rescue. And the lightning of scorn that flashed in her eyes struck the fancy band of his hat, ran down his silk shirt, swept each of the silver constellations that spangled his chaps, seemed even to go behind him and scorch the monograms on his silver spurs before darting back to his face and burning him to a crisp!

"Anyhow," she cried, each word a lash to make Dare writhe, "I do *my* paradin' in private! I don't get out an' make a holy show of myself. I should care if you laugh, you—you *prairie sheik!*"

CHAPTER II

"DON'T TAKE THE CUCKOO!"

SLOW red stained through the bronze of Dare's cheek. But the smart to his vanity was nothing to his remorse that he had hurt. It had been such a let-down to find that it was not a princess at all, but just a slim, little wisp of a girl playing grown-up in this spooky old house; that the purple robe was nothing but an old Navajo blanket she had draped about her, and the diadem, just lupines she had picked out in the garden and put in her hair. That was why he had laughed. Not at how she looked now—facing him across the dim, old hall, her little chin high, her eyes defiant, and so pitifully proud and ashamed, in a faded calico slip that was none too clean, and bare feet.

"I wasn't laughin' at you"—the cowboy's sincerity was not to be doubted—"but at my own self! How this ol' house made me feel. How you fooled me. Why, I rated you right up with the picture cards!"

Joy lighted her face, and she asked breathlessly, as slowly she crossed to him: "Honest, did I act like a lady?"

"Lady!" Dare scorned the word. "Say, you acted a heap more ladyfied than any lady I ever met—bar none!"

To his dismay, that upset her all over again.

"I—I reckon it ain't no use," she said hopelessly,

as he stepped out of the door so she could come through. "I reckon you have to be born a lady to be one natural."

He could not see what difference it made if you did. But he saw plainly that it made a big difference to her. And he was mute with pity, as she sat down on the edge of the gallery, an arm about one of the sagging old pillars, her dark head bent upon it, and her sad eyes fixed on the shadowy court. He knew she had forgotten that he was on earth. Far too interested to be overlooked that way, he sat down beside her, asking curiously:

"Where'd you learn to act like that?"

"In 'The Fatal Wedding' "—she was too discouraged to look up—"an' other books. Pop gets 'em by the bundle in trade. In movies, too, I study hard."

Vastly interested, Dare pursued "Who's Missus Hutchins?"

Again her cheeks unfurled red banners of shame, and her fingers dropped to her skimpy dress, busying themselves putting in tucks. "She runs the dry-goods store over at Sundown."

Remembering in what an unladylike way she had treated the lady who was supposed to have delivered a dress, Dare mischievously pressed: "Why'd you high-hat her? To say nothin' of upsettin' her!"

The grimy little hand took another plait.

"She called me a name!" then flashed the girl, with spirit. "Oh, it was true, all right, but she didn't *need* to do it! She wasn't tellin' me anything I didn't know. I just went in her old store to get some buttons an' a paper of pins, an' was lookin' around—it don't hurt to look—when I heard her tell the clerk to keep her eyes on that—wagon tramp!"

"Why, the ol' hellion!" blazed Dare, so whole-heartedly echoing her previously expressed opinion of the lady in question that they both laughed. And it was like sunshine to dispel the atmosphere of storm that had lain between them.

Suddenly, now, it struck Dare as fully as strange that he should find her here in the melancholy ruins of Corral de Terra, as though she had been the princess. And by way of earning her confidence, he gave her his. He told her who he was, and how he was traveling foot-loose and free, and was not going to stop until a "whole flock of things" happened to him. And then he asked her what her name was.

A little defiantly, as though in fear of his laughing again, she told him.

"Albuquerque—Albuquerque Boone."

Slowly he repeated it, trying to make it fit the little gypsy beside him, when, defensively, she struck in. "It was the best pop could do! An' if you think of the fix he was in—with me just a month old, an' mom just buried, an' him havin' to drive the *Santa Maria,* with me howlin' like a painter for milk, an' mom——"

"Whoa!" entreated Dare all at sea, as that good ship had been. "The *Santa Maria?*"

"Our ol' prairie schooner. Pop named it after Columbus' flagship, because he says he's discovered more of America in it than Christopher ever heard tell of! But about my name. Pop was plumb desperate, he says, an' he swore to call me the next name he seen in print. Right then, he drove by the road sign to—— You guessed it, Albuquerque! But he calls me Allie, for short."

That *did* fit her, like the paper on the wall, and Dare told her so. She swayed back, her slim arms locked about her slim, bare ankles, smiling a gamin-ish little smile to herself.

"It could have been worse," she admitted, letting him in on the joke, "as pop never fails to remind me when I kick. For the next town he come to was Turquesa—an' then I'd have been Turk, or Tur-key, an' I'd sure hate that."

Again their merry laughter routed the funereal silence that hung over the place. And Dare, inter-estedly studying Allie in the pale light, decided she was not pretty—not any raving beauty. But she was cute—he had no other words to express her singular, heart-stirring appeal—cute as a kitten's ear. And she had something other girls didn't have—he didn't know what. He didn't know much about other girls. But Allie—— Though Dare had met her but a mo-ment ago, though he left her forever the next, he knew he'd never forget Allie Boone!

"I was mean," she said suddenly, "to call you names. Jealous mean."

That was all right, he told her, sheepishly dusting his chaps. "Reckon I do look like a peacock. But when my ship come in, I bought every last thing I'd ever wished for, an' th' consequences are what you're gazin' at. Purty awful, I guess."

She assured him it was not and, shyly reaching over, felt his silken sleeve. "I—I wisht I had a dress like that." Sudden wistfulness clouded her eyes. "That color, too. An' stockin's to match. An' slip-pers! But—oh, gee-gosh!" she sighed deeply.

"Wishin' never got me anything, but I keep doin' it. Go through the same rigmarole every night—'Star light, star bright, very first star I seen to-night'— you know. Nothing ever comes of it. Reckon I don't hold my mouth right."

Her smile then seemed to take right hold of Dare's heart and wring it. And he asked her what she would do if her ship came in? Thinking, of course, she would get the new clothes, he was astonished by the ready vehemence with which she panted: "Buy Corral de Terra!"

"Buy this ol' wreck! For Pete's sake, why?" cried Dare. Then, grinning at what he thought he knew: "To git even with Missus Hutchins?"

"No!" she cried passionately. "To fix it up—take the curse off it! Make a home of it! Live in it, an' stop bein' a—wagon tramp!"

Inanely, to hide his pity, Dare asked: "Don't you like travelin'?"

"How do I know?" she countered, with a little shrug of despair. "I never done anything else. I was born in a wagon, an' brought up in a wagon. Pop says I'd die if I was tied to a house. He says most folks is slaves to a house. But I'd rather be a slave to a house than a wagon! An' I'm always happiest when we come back to Corral de Terra."

Dare was surprised. "Then you've been here before?"

"Most every year of my life. We always camp here when we come through the Los Lobos Range. You see, pop's a trader. He buys worn-out horses in the cities we go through, takes 'em to the country, an' gets 'em in shape, and then we traipse around swappin' 'em off. "We got a bunch down here now." She rose abruptly.

"Say," she invited, "if you're not in a rush, come down to camp a spell. Pop will be glad to see you."

The alacrity with which Dare accepted proved that he must have found six weeks of strange trails rather lonely—or showed how completely Allie had captured his fancy. He was up in an instant, saying, as they walked around the house to where he'd left Check:

"Funny I didn't see your camp when I come in."

"You couldn't—it's behind them cottonwoods way down there by the old creek."

Something in her tone made him aware of a change in her. And he knew that Allie regretted her invitation—didn't want him to visit their camp. So keenly did he feel this that he made up his mind to offer some excuse and ride on. But, catching Check by the bridle and turning him back, he saw that, for the second time, she had forgotten him.

She stood in the rank weeds, looking up at the grim, old house, her hands clasped, and her face rapt.

"If *it* had a wish," gravely she whispered, hearing his step, "don't you think it would be to have folks in it? Don't you suppose it gets lonesome—settin' here by the side of the road—looked down on by folks?"

The full force of her meaning was incomprehensible to Dare Devlyn as yet. But he thought how many slights she must have suffered to give her a sympathetic understanding like that.

"You funny kid," he muttered, a lump in his throat.

Quick to resent that reflection on her maturity,

or the pity he had not been able to hide, she retorted: "Oh, you're no Methuselah yourself!"

He proved it by the sheer boyishness of his answer: "I'm twenty-two!"

She gave him a droll, little, superior smile. "Well, I'm seventeen! Every one knows that's old for a woman."

Seventeen! Dare could not believe her a day over fifteen at best. Still—*a woman!* He turned away to hide a grin. And when he looked back she was staring at Check.

Every one stared at Dare's paint pony, for Check was a marvel of beauty, as well as of speed. His colors—milk-white and jet-black—were laid over him in a strikingly zigzag pattern of checks that drew every eye. But no one had ever looked at him as Allie did now.

Slowly she went up to him and walked about him; slowly she ran an awed finger over the saddle's silver tracery, over the silver on breast collar and bridle. Then slowly she looked up at Dare. The admiration he expected to see in her eyes was not there. Only dread—deep, nameless dread.

"Gee, but pop *will* be glad to see you!" she said strangely.

Without another word she hurried ahead of him, down the long slope back of the barn where the cottonwoods were. And Dare, leading Check, saw a clearing beyond the trees, and in it an old covered wagon—the *Santa Maria*. It had been set up on blocks, and the wheels removed and placed in the creek, that the rattly old spokes might expand with the moisture; and beyond the creek were the horses she had mentioned—the scrubbiest lot he had ever seen, the like he hoped never to see again!

To a man who was a lover of fine horseflesh, as Dare was, and who had a deep affection for "man's faithful friend," the spectacle of these battered old hulks—equine tramps, they might be called—was inexpressibly saddening.

There were horses with broken wind, broken hoofs, broken hearts; horses with ringbone, spavins, and stringhalt. The lame and blind and sick and sore— all were here, and more, worn out by hard work on hard pavement and sold for a song, or given for riddance, to know again—what must be heaven for them—the touch of soft, cool earth on crippled feet, the taste of growing grass, the freedom of open range, until, strengthened and healed by nature—they were sold back into slavery again.

Now, Dare's sober gaze, coming back from the feeding wrecks, took in the dingy, tattered, old tent, pitched between the wagon and stream; and, before it, a great pile of horse blankets, harness, all the unsightly paraphernalia of camp. Suddenly Dare understood Allie's rebellion against it all—her wish to escape, if only in dreams. For wherever the old wagon stopped, wherever the old tent was pitched, this same squalid clutter of things surrounded her, made up her life, was home.

Thinking of her, as he threaded the last of the cottonwood trunks to where a genial-looking, bewhiskered, spry little man was manipulating a frying pan over a crackling camp fire, Dare was startled to find Allie beside him again.

"Say"—earnestly she looked up at him, painfully struggling for words—"I ought to tell you. I—I like pop a heap—but folks say he ain't worth a whoop on a pile of rocks. Usually, I don't say nothing—it's dog eat dog. But you—I seen you first, an' —seems like I couldn't stand to have pop skin a friend."

Her hand plucked his sleeve, and her voice dropped to a whisper. "Dare," she warned, to his utter mystification, "whatever you do—*don't take the cuckoo!*"

CHAPTER III

TO say that Allie's pop was glad to see his chance caller is putting it mildly. When his ear caught the tinkle of silver and he looked up to see the gorgeously caparisoned cowboy and horse, as his appreciative gaze took in the full splendor of Check, his dazed expression said plainly that it must be true, for he was seeing it, but it wasn't possible, nevertheless. And, dropping the skillet like a live coal, he stepped energetically out to meet Dare, a miracle of self-possession in his frayed blue jeans and soiled denim shirt.

"It's Dare Devlyn, pop," briefly Allie explained, running to rescue the frying pan from the flames.

"My name's Boone," heartily stated the trader, "though I'm commonly called by the entitlement, 'Swap.'" He seized Dare's hand, pumped his arm vigorously, and formalities were at an end. For with Swap Boone getting acquainted was no slow and tortuous process, but a spontaneous act. And an hour at his camp fire was the establishment of a long, long friendship—to be traded on accordingly.

"Travelin'?" he sociably queried, his eye on Check.

"Yeah," Dare grinned, sizing him up for a humbug, but liking him, nevertheless.

"Profit or pleasure?"

"Fun—just hittin' the high spots."

Swap nodded. "Ain't apt to be much profit in it," he allowed, as one whose word on that point carried some weight. "As the old sayin' goes: 'Stay put, an' you'll gather moss.' But I never had no aspirations to be a mossback myself. Oh, I reckon I *could* put down a root an' flourish like a green bay tree! But I'll take mine rollin' an' take less."

A sentiment with which Dare coincided. But his glance went to Allie. She was bent over the table—formed by turning back the cover of the grub box and propping it up on a stick. And though she seemed wholly absorbed in the task of stirring batter in a bowl half as big as herself, he had the feeling that she was not missing a word.

"No, thanks." Dare refused the villainous plug Swap was pressing on him. "I inhale mine." And he built a cigarette and lit it, while the trader, wrenching off a generous chew, leisurely strolled around Check.

"Right smart hoss—that."

And Dare modestly owned: "Not bad."

But his pleasure at the compliment gave way to vague uneasiness as the trader ran a practiced hand over the paint's smooth hip, down his satiny, tapering leg, and took an unobtrusive squint at his teeth.

"Nope—not bad, a-tall." Ruminatively, Swap snapped his suspenders—probably the only pair in the Los Lobos Range. And now his eye was hypnotic, his voice persuasive as he asked: "How'll you swap for that bay geldin' nighest the creek?"

Dare glanced around at the pitiful, disjointed rack of bones indicated—the worst in the lot—and back at Swap, smiling broadly. He could not believe that the trader was serious, and was astonished to see that he was. So he said, in a tone meant to nip that idea right in the bud: "Not while I'm conscious!"

Apparently, it was all one to Swap. He insisted that Dare "rest his saddle" and have supper with them. And the cowboy accepted this invitation as well. But he regretted it a dozen times before he sat down to the meal.

For, with praiseworthy persistence, Swap worked on the trade. The contents of the old prairie schooner —which would have done credit to any junk store— were dragged, individually, out to the light, and offered as "boot" between the bay ruin and Check. A moth-eaten buffalo robe, a clothes wringer, and a pair of field glasses that were blind in one eye, were displayed one at a time, with a lecture recounting the peculiar merits of each. And, when each was declined, all three were offered in toto, and a bundle of paper-backed novels thrown in. Even after Dare firmly stated that he was "not on the trade," Swap's eye continued to rove to the paint, cropping near, in a way that showed he was not without hope.

They were lounging now on boxes about the camp fire, shut in from the world by the gathering night. And Dare, watching Allie kneel to take off the kettle, a bare arm thrown up to shield her face from the flames, felt his heart contracting with pity again. This life was fine for a man—for Swap; but it must be hard on a girl—a girl who wanted to be a lady, whose heart was broken because she had been called a wagon tramp, and knew she was! She sure had it in her to amount to something. Why, up there in Corral de Terra, playing lady——

Hearing Swap clear his throat to dicker some more, Dare forestalled him. "Some *hacienda!*" he said, and nodded toward the black bulk of the old house, limned against the sky over the trees.

"Has been," Swap agreed, "all that, an' then some —in its day."

"Funny it's vacant," Dare pursued, "a watered place, too! And even in the Los Lobos, water——"

"Water," dolefully cut in the trader, "won't wash out blood!"

A shiver ran over Dare, as when he had entered the garden up there.

"Blood"—somehow Swap's tone invoked a whole sea of it—"is on the ol' house. Likewise, men say the curse of Heaven is on it! 'Hell's Hip Pocket,' they call it! It's hoodooed worse'n Friday, number thirteen, or a alley plumb full of black cats!"

"You mean"—Dare's eyes strained on the black hulk up there—"that it's haunted, Swap?"

"If it ain't, it ought to be! But, great Goliath, do you mean to say you ain't heard tell of Corral de Terra?"

"Something," Dare told him, but he could not remember what. "All I recollect is that it links up with Jessimer."

"It was the home ranch of the Jessimer family— an' the death of it!" Swap, a born story-teller, loved to tell a story next to making a trade, and was, beyond words, happy when engaged in both. Now he leaned forward, his face in the shadows, his tone as unconsciously theatrical as Allie's had been.

"There was three Jessimers, brothers—Joe, Pete, an' Lynne—as wild an' reckless a crew as ever the Southwest produced. They run their herds from El Capitan to the Sulphur Desert, east and west, an' from horizon to horizon, north an' south. So they was natural leaders in the range war what depopulated this section thirty years back.

"But the fight got out of hand—what with both sides, cattle an' sheep, bringin' in hired guns. An' one black day the combined forces of Los Lobos sheepmen cornered the Jessimer cohorts at Corral de Terra. Right up there"—he pointed to the grim blot on the sky line—"the Jessimer boys made their last stand. There was two score of saddles emptied forever in that fight. When help come—— Sure you ain't thought better of that last trade?"

Dare was positive.

Swap resumed, with no slightest change of tone: "When help come—in the shape of more cowmen—Lynne Jessimer was holdin' the fort alone. They found him a-standin' in the court, a-pumpin' lead from two guns, so hot that they fired the grass when he fell—with a dozen bullet holes in him. They found Pete Jessimer face up in the yard—dead as a mackerel, an' Joe stretched out on the gallery—plumb dead!"

Swap paused dramatically in the telling. The river splashed against the wheels of the *Santa Maria*. The fire crackled. The horses contentedly munched the grass. Allie's bare feet passed noiselessly between table and camp fire. And Dare's heart beat almost audibly at this tale of supreme adventure, as his mind leaped now to the memory that had eluded him, yet colored his thoughts up there.

"The shootin' an' the tumult died. The smoke an' smell of powder drifted out the broken doors, an' Corral de Terra was the wreck you seen, with the windows shot out, the casin's smashed to splinters, an' enough lead buried in them walls to sink a battleship. But Lynne, the last Jessimer——" Abruptly, then, as Dare breathlessly waited for the fate of the last Jessimer, Swap hinted: "The bay geldin', an' that team of grays behind you, for the paint!"

With fierce impatience, and not so much as a glance behind, Dare prompted: "Lynne?"

"Lynne got the best of his wounds," went on the imperturbable trader, "an' set out to avenge his brothers. At the head of a wild band of night riders who——"

"The *Lobos!*" Dare's dark eyes glowed, as his soul fired at that memory.

"The Lobos," solemnly echoed Swap. "With them at his back, he set out to wipe the sheepmen off the Los Lobos Range. In the dead of night, their movements a dead secret to all but themselves, they'd swooped down on sheep camp or ranch, shoutin' the battle cry of vengeance! Many were killed. More fled the country in terror of them. An' Lynne had gone a long way toward fulfillin' his purpose, when the country rose up agin' the bloodshed an' had the soldiers sent in. An indictment was got out for Lynne—the only member of that band they knowed for certain—but he——" Swap fished his jack-knife out of his pocket, picked up a fagot of cotton-wood cut for the fire, and meditatively, *maddeningly,* to the cowboy, started to whittle.

"But he?" prompted Dare, tense with interest.

Swap looked up mildly. "Why, he disappeared. Nobody knows where. Some say he's been seen here, some say there. But nobody ever found any-body who actually seen him. But, now an' then—as with sad frequency happens in these wild Nimbres —when some hombre runs onto the skull of a human an' a rusted ol' firin' piece in the grass, he thinks hard of the last Jessimer—Lynne."

There was a long silence, in which Swap whittled. Then Dare demanded, "Ain't any one lived in the ol' place since?"

Swap shook his head. "When Kit Kress set up in the land-office business, he hung out a shingle offerin' Corral de Terra for sale. Nobody knows on what authority. Nobody asked. Folks ain't in the habit of questioning ol' Kit's authority! He wasn't always an agent, see? A busted kneecap was what laid him up. Anyhow, nobody wanted to buy it. You couldn't give that place to a Los Lobos man —not after all the blood what's been spilled up there. Shame, too," he said, as an afterthought, "for it's a gold mine just as it sets! Got a knife, pard?"

Dare had, and he produced it—an expensive, stag-handled hunting knife. Laying his own on a box, Swap took it, admiringly turned it over a time or two in his palm, then leisurely tried out each blade on the stick.

"How's there a gold mine in Corral de Terra?" Dare entreated.

"That," philosophized the itinerant trader, "is where travel comes in. Nothin's so broadenin' as travel. It shows you how much folks is alike the world over. How the best of 'em is cat curious respectin' the deeds of the worst of 'em. Take this ol' ranch—— Fair knife. How'll you swap?"

"Even"—Dare was exasperated—"if you'll go on!"

"Take this ol' place," said Swap, speeded up considerably by this small success, "an' advertise it! Advertise the trouble it's been through. Cash in on the frailties of human nature! Cash in on the name of Jessimer! Folks'll stampede this ranch, an' pay handsome for the privilege of sleepin' in the ol' Jessimer home, if they have to be hung up by the thumbs."

"A dude ranch!" The cowboy's eyes flashed disdain.

And Swap, incensed by this light dismissal of his pet idea, sprang up and circled the fire thrice. "Hotel! Tavern! Road house! Inn!" he exploded, striking a dramatic pose before Dare. "Any name 'u'd smell as sweet to me! Advertise! Then set back an' rake in the chips. They'll come in flocks. The higher the charge, the bigger the flock. If that won't bring 'em, warn 'em there's more trouble of the same order brewin'! You couldn't keep 'em off with a shotgun then!"

"But," objected Dare simply, "there ain't! This is the tamest country I ever was in!"

Swap gave him a queer look. "On the surface, mebbe." His gentle correction thrilled Dare strangely. "But you don't know what's simmerin' under. *Wait!* Wait, till the hate an' fury what's gathered these thirty years busts through the crust! Right this minit, Cull Cole's a-rangin' sheep toward the Upper Rio! Right this minit, Gid Perkins' riders are watchin' the river like hawks! An' the sheep must go on—for their range is a dust heap!"

"I seen that, Swap."

"You think the Los Lobos is tame!" Swap couldn't get over it. "Say, there's ol' codgers tucked away in every nook an' cranny of it what's been a-smolderin' more years than you've been a mortal! An' they'll sure go up, if the sheepmen try to take that range north of Rio. Partic'ly, if some hombre takes over

Corral de Terra, like I told you. That's sheep range by the ol' truce. But the men what compromised it wouldn't have allotted it that a way—crowded sheep so close to a cow ranch—if Corral de Terra hadn't been abandoned at the time. If it comes back —— *Tame?* It's dynamite! I'm tellin' you, man!"

Moodily, Swap resumed his pacing. Allie, who had come to call them to supper, forgot to do so. And Dare's brain ran wild. He'd been born too late to get in on the old excitement, but the Los Lobos was dynamite still! It would sure be exciting if it exploded again, and excitement was rare—as he had come far enough without seeing any to know. You couldn't buy it. But you might—just by taking over Corral de Terra——

"Is that," he asked suddenly, "why you ain't made a gold mine out of it, Swap?"

"Holy catamount, no!" Swap denied feelingly. "It's lack of cash. It would take a fortune—ten thousand dollars"—with all due reverence, he named the sum— "to do it right!"

And, to himself, there in the fire glow, Dare mused audibly: "I've got ten thousand bucks."

Allie started, that look of dread leaping again to her eyes. Swap's knees slowly buckled beneath him, and he sank back on his box.

"You have got—*ten—thousand—bucks?*" gasped Swap.

Startlingly, as Dare affirmed it, the trader bounced up and rushed past him, dived head first into the *Santa Maria,* backed out like a crab, and came toward them with his arms full of something.

Allie's black eyes shot warning at Dare, and he caught her tense whisper: "Haywire!"

Then Swap was back. Placing his burden on the box he had occupied, he removed the quilt from about it as tenderly as though it swaddled an infant, revealing to Dare's stupefied gaze a battered old walnut case containing an eight-day clock.

In absolute silence, as though confident that this article could speak for itself, Swap wound the old relic, placed the hands at the hour of three, and stepped back, rapture under his whiskers and his eyes on Dare. And nervously as the cowboy had jumped at the scream of the red-tailed hawk in the crumbling court, even more nervously did he jump as the mangy little bird sprang out of its tiny house on top of the clock, lustily sang, *"Cuckoo! Cuckoo! Cuckoo!"* and bobbed in again, clapping its little door behind it.

Huskily, as one breathes a sacrifice almost too great to put into words, Swap Boone whispered: "The gray team, the bay geldin', *an' the cuckoo,* for the paint!"

This seemed to Dare so ridiculous that he laughed wildly, as he had laughed in the old house to Allie's shame. But her expression was one of relief now. for a weight seemed to lift from her as he gasped: "You must think I'm cuckoo too!"

And yet, when this night had passed into history— red sequel to the Jessimer story—Dare's shame that he had laughed at the old cuckoo clock was greater than Allie's had been!

They sat down to the corn pones, bacon, and hominy that had been allowed to get cool. All through the meal, Swap enlarged upon the possibilities of Corral de Terra with an enthusiasm he could not have exceeded had he been the agent, Kit Kress.

It was, he assured the opulent cowboy, the chance
of his lifetime, and opportunity must be seized by
the forelock, since it was bald behind. Allie said
nothing. But her big, black eyes burned out of the
shadows, haunting Dare.

Gazing up at the storied old ruin, now bathed in
the ghostly radiance of the early moon, Dare dreamed.
And in his dreams he saw Corral de Terra, not as it
was—ruined, forsaken—but as it could be, with the
buildings repaired and peopled, a hive of industry,
and the ground rumbling again to the low thunder
of a herd. He saw himself in the midst of it all,
master of it all, surrounded by folks as hungry for
excitement as he—and his chief task to manufacture
excitement for them!

And he saw Allie—first and last, he saw Allie!—
moving through the misty old hall as he'd first seen
her—as he was destined in his inmost heart ever to
see her—not in the purple robe, of course, but
dressed up and on her dignity, greeting his guests.

It was late when Dare finished with dreams and
rose to go.

"Well," he said, his regret as genuine as theirs,
"I'd best be moseyin'."

As Swap silently went for Check, Dare held out
his hand. "Adios, Allie!"

She gave him hers—such a rough little hand.
"Good-by, Dare."

Then he took leave of Swap, swung up on the
paint horse, and rode off through the trees. But
before the boughs had quite closed around him, he
looked back.

Allie stood just as he had left her—a forlorn,
little figure, outlined by the flames; but he knew,

without seeing, that her fingers were taking more tucks. And he thought how fine and honest she was—afraid he'd be skinned by pop. He thought of her making her wish to the stars at night, with no hope of its coming true. And he wondered what she was thinking. How unfair life could be? That he, who didn't want it, should have everything *she* wanted—money to buy a home, help her to be the somebody she wanted to be? And was she really seeing him leave—or was it her every hope and ambition in life that was riding away?

CHAPTER IV

GO SLOW!

THE door of Sundown's one real-estate office stood hospitably open, so as to impede neither the morning sunshine nor any possible business. And through it, Kit Kress might be seen, tilted back in his swivel chair, his crippled leg eased over one end of his desk, a brown-paper cigarette dead on his lips, thinking—Heaven knows what!

There were many who would have given a pretty penny for old Kit's thoughts, particularly when he cast them back over the years before he had opened this office in Sundown. For, as Swap said, Kit had not always been the calm, inscrutable man of business they knew. His every mood and mannerism betokened the range man. The marks of alkali, wind, and sun in his shrewd old face, the look of far horizons in his steady, gray eyes, the very set of his lean, straight form, branded him as a rider.

It was rumored, in fact, that he had ridden with Lynne Jessimer in the terrible vengeance raids. A rumor, by the way, circulated about most Los Lobos men over sixty whose sympathies had been on the Jessimer side. In Kit's case, the rumor went farther.

When the soldiers who had hemmed in the last Jessimer in a mountain retreat returned to report his escape, they lauded the courage of a second rider who had made the break with Lynne, deliberately acted as a shield for him, and, though hard hit, contrived his escape. And it was said that this nervy rider had been Kit Kress, that it was in his last service to Jessimer that he had suffered the shattered kneecap that had demoted him from saddle to desk, and to the handling of such innocuous weapons as leases and deeds. Be that as it may—the personnel of that wild band was known only to the Lobos themselves.

Certainly, Kit Kress alone knew the answer to the still burning question—whether Lynne Jessimer was living or dead. For his first listing, on opening this office, had been the home ranch of the Jessimers', for whom he had power of attorney. But whether he acted for Lynne, or his heirs, was never ascertained. When taxes fell due on Corral de Terra, he paid them personally, and in every way kept the owner's identity hidden.

Thirty years ago, he had nailed the sign to the old ranch gate. In thirty years it had brought no inquiries. Long ago, Kit had ceased to expect any. Old-timers, who in hot-blooded youth had been ranged either for or against it, had kept alive its dark history, so that years had added not only to its general deterioration, but to its sinister repute.

So this June morn, as Kit sat thinking, his thoughts died a violent death when the most fancy dressed young puncher he had ever laid eyes on stepped in and inquired about Corral de Terra!

For moments, Kit Kress stared at Dare Devlyn, as though at a specter materialized out of the black thoughts that had been in his mind. Then his lips twisted soundlessly. "Corral de Terra?" he asked at length.

"Yeah," Dare grinned. "You're agent for it, ain't you? The sign said that——"

"Why, I—I guess I am——" stuttered old Kit. "Great horned toad, sure I'm agent for it! But Corral de Terra—Lord!"

So downright was his surprise that Dare laughed, and Kit took an instant liking to him. Shrewd judge of human nature that he was, the agent sized up a man by his laugh. He despised and distrusted a smirker. A man stingy with his smile was bound to be small in more ways than one But this lad laughed with his eyes, his mouth, his whole slim, sinewy being, and so infectiously that Kit, stunned as he was, found himself joining in. Then he put his game leg under the desk, shakily applied a match to his dead cigarette, and got down to business.

"Cowman?" he asked, as a matter of course.

"I'll say!"

"Did you aim to buy—or lease?"

"Buy—if the terms are right."

"They *will* be!" Kress assured his one and only prospect for Corral de Terra

And so "right" did he make them that in an astonishingly short lapse of time Dare found himself signing an agreement whereby, for a consideration of ten thousand dollars—two thousand down, and the balance on easy payments—the historic old ranch passed into his hands. And he pocketed the document, confident in the knowledge that he had eight thousand left to repair the house, buy stock, and put into operation the numerous schemes that he had hatched in the night and that were running away with him.

"By the way," Kress said, as they shook hands on

the deal, "there's a tramp trader camped out there now. Do you want I should run him off, or will you?"

"Lord, no!" exclaimed the boy fervently. "Not if you mean Swap! I'm hirin' him."

Unexpectedly, Kit's eyes twinkled. "Does Swap know it?" he asked. When Dare admitted that he didn't—yet, Kit's twinkle deepened and he said:

"Waal, I'll bet a cowbell you don't, if Swap knows it!"

"I'll take you!" Dare said earnestly, as Kress followed him out. "Why, Swap's gotta stay! He's part of my plan."

At that, the agent—singularly interested in this fine-looking puncher who had appeared so mysteriously, displaying unlimited cash and courage in taking over the hoodoed ranch—frankly asked:

"Just what is your plan? Tell me it's none of my business, if you like, son, but it would ease my conscience a heap to know how you aimed to make the old place pay."

Thinking of Allie, Dare colored deeply. Here, in the broad light of day, after the unromantic atmosphere of the agent's office, his first motive struck him as sentimental in the last degree. However, his second was equally strong.

"I'm goin' to cash in on its wild reputation," he said, enthusiasm lighting up his face. "Of course, I'll stock it—for Corral de Terra must be a bonafide cow ranch. But, first and last, it's thrills I'm sellin'!" And he went on to outline his plan, much as Swap had done to him.

Kress did not interrupt. Nor, when Dare was

done did he make any comment; indeed, he discon-
certed the boy by the lack of it.

"Here's the idea!" Impetuously, Dare defended
his plan. "All my life I've been crazy for one rip-
snortin', wild-an'-woolly, blood-an'-thundery, good
time! So has every one—deep down inside. But
things don't happen any more. You gotta make 'em
happen! So I'm goin' to sell folks that kind of a
time. I'll bait 'em here with the old excitement at
Corral de Terra, promise 'em more of the same,
make 'em think it's an adventure just bein' here!
Though I don't know how I'll make that promise
good—on this sleepy, dead range. But I sure aim
to wake it!"

Suddenly, then, Kress spoke, and somberly, with
a tremor that stirred Dare's blood as a foretaste of
the excitement he craved.

"Lord pity us one, an' pity us all, if ever the Los
Lobos wakes up!"

To his overwhelming dismay, he saw joy flash
in the cowboy's eyes. And all at once he would have
given a lot to have that deed back! Better never have
sold Corral de Terra—better, a thousand times better, let it go on to wrack and ruin. But a man had
a right to do as he pleased with his own ranch.

"Son," he said gravely, "I'd be the last one to dis-
courage you, but there's things you ought to know.
Corral de Terra's the key ranch in a big range dispute that was never rightly settled. There's a large
section of range, north of the Upper Rio, that, due
to its proximity to Corral de Terra, should have been
allotted to beef. But no one was ranchin' the place
at the time, an' it didn't seem likely there ever would
be—so it was apportioned to sheep. Cowmen pro-

tested it, an' sheepmen never claimed it—knowin' they'd have to fight to git it, an' havin' plenty of feed without. But now—range is gittin' scarce. Sheep will have to take that section, or leave the Los Lobos. Cowmen will fight sheep ever goin' on that block—seein' it as an enterin' wedge to their own range. An', since Corral de Terra will benefit most by keepin' sheep off, its owner will be expected to back the cowmen up strong in that fight. Now—I'll give your money back if you like."

His heart skipped a beat at Dare's reckless laugh. "No chance! I'm sure gittin' a bargain, Kress."

"More than you bargained for, mebbe," old Kit warned. "Son, excitement's a crop that grows wild in Los Lobos soil. Might easily kill out everything else. Go slow." And even more gravely, he added: "Go *mighty* slow."

But when was youth ever warned? Eager to accomplish his many errands in town, to get back and tell Allie that he had bought Corral de Terra, and that she and Swap had a home, Dare said, with another handshake: "So long."

"So long," echoed Kit wearily. "An' good luck!" But his good wishes died in his throat.

And as Dare rode off up the street to unwittingly set Sundown by the ears with news that the ill-fated old ranch had a tenant at last—Kit limped inside and slumped back at his desk. He sat there long, his face as gray as his shaggy mane, his eyes journeying over the sunlit plains to that far peak, towering above all other peaks in the Nimbres Range, to El Capitan—the mountain that had looked down on such fearful scenes of blood and strife. At last he whis-

pered, a sudden constriction making his whisper thick:
"Corral de Terra's come to life again!"

A long, shuddering sigh ran through him, and
fearfully, as to some unseen presence, he cried:

"Lynne, ol' pal, I hope the dust we raised in our
own hot youth has plumb settled! Please Heaven,
this rash lad don't raise it again!"

Then into his mind flashed Gid Perkins' face, as
he had seen it but yesterday—desperate, set—and his
brain rang again to the driven intensity in the old
cowman's voice, as he had cried:

"Kit, the lion an' the lamb can't cuddle down
together much longer in the Los Lobos. If Cull Cole
drives his danged woollies north of Rio—Kit, I can't
hold in! Why *should* I? What are we these days—
men, mice, or long-tailed rats! Was the spawn of
men wiped from the earth with the Jessimers? By
gravy, I'm goin' to rise up—be a man!"

On and on Kit's mind ran—over things that might
raise the old dust and precipitate the calamity he
feared. And he thought of a thousand things that
could, yet they numbered not the thing that did!

CHAPTER V

ALL that was earthly of Allie Boone was curled in the shade of the *Santa Maria*. But her imaginative spirit had escaped to high planes of romance, found between the paper backs of "The Fatal Wedding," her textbook and guide. With dark head bent over the pages, absorbedly chewing her cheap, yellow beads, Allie was studying hard.

"Lady Charlotte floated down the marble staircase in a cloud of silk," she read. "Pale, proud, peerless beauty!"

How did one float down stairs? She couldn't practice that, for Corral de Terra didn't have a staircase. But she bet she could float, she could *fly*, in a cloud of silk. It was hard to do anything much in old overalls.

"Gliding from the palms"—she could do that, glide—"Sir Basil took his fair mistress upon his arm, bending on her a look more potent than elixir——" She knew what that meant now! That had been an elixir-ous look Dare had bent on her up in the court last night, when he said, "You funny kid!" Dare was as handsome as Sir Basil, too! And he'd gone. Every one she ever liked went on—or she had to leave them. The only friends she could keep were these—in books. Fiercely brushing away the tear that splashed on the page, she resumed: "And the soul of Lady Charlotte melted in——"

A sound struck her ear, bringing her back to the miserable realities of the river camp. Tossing her short, black curls out of her eyes, Allie looked up to see four black-and-white legs weaving through the cottonwood trunks. And she sprang up, clutching the book to her breast, joy and surprise making stars of her eyes, as the rider—to her more gallant and chivalrous than all her heroes, Sir Basil, Galahad, or young Lochinvar—came toward her, wildly waving his black sombrero, shouting excitedly:

"Allie, I've bought the ol' ranch!"

Dare could not wait till he got there, and his news brought Swap up from the creek on a run, with the bottle of liniment he'd been rubbing on the stiff leg of the bay ruin he'd tried to trade in for Check.

"It's mine, Allie! An', Swap, I'm goin' to do just like you said! Made a big start already. Got an army of men, tools an' material, comin' to-morrow, an' a wagonload of stuff on the way right now! An' I got a line on a hombre what's sellin' out, an' I'm dickerin' for his whole outfit an' herd. An' I'm goin' to git bad horses, an' good riders, an' stage a Wild West show for the folks. An'—oh, criminy, I don't know what-all I am goin' to do!"

He slid to the ground, straddled the tongue of the *Santa Maria,* and looking up at their blank faces, babbled on about what he had done.

"I hunted up the newspaper man in Sundown, an' got him to write a lotta come-hither stuff. Had him lay it on thick—about the hair-raisin' times this ranch has been through, an' how the Los Lobos is dynamite yet. Told 'em we was expectin' range trouble, an' couldn't take but a limited number. Told 'em they come at their own risk, like you said, an' first come, first served, an' all that! An' he's sendin' it to all the papers back East. An' if we're goin' to be ready to take in boarders by the middle of next month, like it says, we sure gotta hump ourselves some!"

Breathless, he waited for their reaction, but they were as breathless as he. They just stared at him—Swap hugging his liniment bottle, and Allie her book. The trader was awed dumb by the magnitude of his own proposition. His was the mind to conceive big projects, but he lacked the nerve to carry them through. And Allie—to have saved her life, Allie couldn't have spoken.

"It's your home as much as mine!" Dare told them, and he thought it was worth ten thousand of any man's money to have brought that look to her eyes. "You're to move in the minit I get things ready. Which'll be pronto! It's in surprisin' good shape. Them adobe walls is three feet through. They'll last for another million years. We'll have to fix the floors, put in new windows, an' hang new doors—but nothin' that takes long!"

"That's right kind of you," Swap managed at last.

It was nothing of the kind, Dare declared. There wouldn't be any kick in doing it for himself. Besides, he'd need a woman to look after the house.

"That's your job, Allie!" Gee, she was twice as cute—in them little blue overalls, and that string of beads—as she'd been last night! Just a little "star light, star bright" herself, who would shine any old where! "You're boss of the *hacienda!* Kick Swap an' me out if we git in your way Fix it up pretty. Do every last thing you ever dreamed of doin' to it!"

"*Oh!*" That one rapturous syllable conveyed all the thanks in the world.

"An' I'm payin' you for doin' it, savvy?" He had thought of everything. "So you can buy a red velvet rag to wear in the garden, a dress like my shirt, an' them slippers an' things—an' go in town an' plumb pulverize Missus Hutchins! But you ain't to work none—not clean, or cook. I'll have a house crew for that. You ain't to lift a finger to a thing that ain't lady's work! Meet our boarders at the door with a smile, an' send 'em home the same. Give class to the place!"

"Oh!" Her joy was so keen that it was pain. And Dare, blinded by its glow in her face, turned to the unilluminated visage of Swap.

"You better run this wagon alongside the ol' buckboard in thet shed up there—two mighty fine relics to start! Then turn these poor plugs out on the range, an' we'll pitch right in. You got a job from this minit, Swap!"

"Oh!" Swap said, too, but with a difference. "What's my job?"

That was the spirit, the cowboy made mental applause. Kress had lost his bet, and Dare was a cowbell ahead already.

"There's more to do than you can shake a stick at!" he assured Swap. "No end of jobs!" And, with an enthusiasm that prevented his seeing that it was not shared, he enumerated them: "Corrals to build, fences to fix, ditches to dig——"

The rumble of the wagon that had followed him out, with the things of which he stood in most immediate need, was heard in the court. And Dare took hasty leave of the Boones.

Changing his fancy dress for the flannel shirt and khaki pants he had bought in town, he pitched in. In the kitchen of Corral de Terra he set up the stove that had come on the wagon. He repaired a bunk in the best end of the bunk house, and unrolled his blankets. He temporarily mended the least dilapidated corral for Check. Then, remembering a hundred things he had forgotten to do in town, he made another trip.

It was dark when he returned, and too late to go down to Swap's camp. So, opening a can of baked beans, another of yellow clings, he made coffee, dined like a king under his own rooftree, and went to bed. He lay awake for hours, while his mind worked on, building more plans.

And he blessed old Aunt Martha, who had left all that money to him with no strings attached. She had never seen him. She had left it to him to spite the rest of the family whom she *had* seen. But it sure was a grand and glorious feeling to be able to help other folks—settle Swap down and give Allie a home. He liked them both. It was most like having a family. "We'll put the ol' cuckoo over the mantelpiece," was his last waking plan.

Bird songs in the sycamores woke Dare early and bright. And he lay for a moment between sleeping and waking, knowing somehow that this was not just any ordinary morning, but not certain why. Then it came to him with a rush and he jumped up and dressed, eager not to miss a moment of it. And when he went out and saw the old house flooded with sungold, his heart almost burst with pride to know

it was his. He was glad it was wrecked! If it had
not been, he could not have touched it. He had got
it as a bargain that staggered him yet. And it was
going to be fun to improve it—exciting, just to work
for himself.

But there was so much to do, he did not know
where to begin. So he did what many a man in the
same position has done—nothing at all. He decided
to go down and talk it over with Swap.

He struck off down the slope, singing as blithely as
the meadow lark on the wall, a song that the old
house called to mind:

"Oh the hinges are of leather,
An' the windows have no glass,
An' the board roof lets the howlin' blizzard in."

And, as he came through the trees to the clearing,
by the creek,

"I can hear the hungry coyote,
As he sneaks up through the grass,
In my little ol' sod shanty on the plai——"

On that note both Dare and his song stopped.
Ecstasy fled his soul. For the old covered wagon,
the miserable horses, the dingy old tent, were gone!
Only the ashes of the breakfast fire—still warm—and
a heap of tin cans, showed that a camp had ever been
there—these, and outgoing tracks, fresh in the bank
of the flashing stream.

Overwhelmed by this discovery, Dare followed
the tracks out to the main road, where they streaked
east. Not just gone to Sundown for grub, or to

trade, but—gone! Swap Boone had folded his tent like an Arab—was rolling again! And Allie——— She had gone without a word of good-by, or thanks. He could not believe it. But it was written in the road, and dumbly he stared at the writing. He was still staring, when a decrepit bay of familiar aspect rounded the bend just ahead, and came in a hitching lope toward him. And on him, a slim, little rider in overalls—*Allie!*

Dare's heart gave a tremendous leap, his elation soared twice as high in the rebound, till he saw that Allie was crying—hopelessly, soddenly, into her horse's mane.

"I thought you'd gone," he cried, catching her bridle.

She lifted a tear-stained face, surprised at meeting him here.

"I am," she said drearily. "I just come back to say good-by. But—I'm gone!"

Then she broke into a wild storm of weeping. Lifting her from the horse, Dare carried her to the shade, where she tore from him, and slowly sank in the grass, sobbing as though her heart would break.

"Allie," he cried, in alarm, "what's wrong? Was Swap sore because I took his idea? He told me to. I done it for you."

"It—ain't—that!" she gasped, sitting up. "He's glad. He says he hopes you'll make good—an' knows you will. But—pop's proud—as Lucifer. Too proud to work! He says it would be a sin an' a shame— for a man of his—s-swappin' ability just to d-dig in a d-ditch———"

"But, holy cow!" protested the boy, giddy with

relief. "He don't *have* to dig. Allie, he don't have to do a blamed thing. He's welcome just to——"

"Pop ain't a sponger," she informed him, with that proud little lift of the chin.

Not knowing what to say or do, Dare pleaded helplessly: "Allie, you can't go! I stayed for you! So we could take the curse off the ol' place—remember?—so you could have a home—like other girls. Why, I—I even had a place for the cuckoo clock!"

She almost smiled then. "I'm glad pop didn't work it off on you, for it only runs five minutes at a windin', Dare. Pop calls it his Jonah. He swapped a blind mare an' a currycomb for it up in Abilene last fall, an' it's the only thing he ever got that he can't swap off. It's kinda took the conceit out of pop—like failin' with you last night. He's been down in the mouth ever since."

She rose then. Sadly she held out her hand. "Well, I'd better be goin', Dare, or I won't catch up." Then the thought of what she was leaving— her chance of a lifetime—of the wretched existence she was going on with, tore her to pieces again, and she threw herself face down on the grass, crying wildly:

"I—I'm plumb sick of it! So sick of the dirt an' grind, so—so ashamed, Dare! Everybody snickers at us. An' I get so lonesome—I want to die half the time! Oh, I wisht I was dead! I wisht I was dead!"

But this storm passed, too, and Dare dried her eyes with his bandanna, though his own eyes needed attention as well. Then he swung her up on the bay, still keeping his arms about her, because it did not seem as though he could let her go.

"I'm glad *you* got Corral de Terra," she whispered.

"I'll be happy just knowin' that, wherever I go. But," with fierce naïveté, "I couldn't stand thinkin' of any other woman fixin' it up!"

"There won't be," he promised, touched by that.

Thrilled by his promise, she impulsively put her arms about him, bent her lips to his in a swift, shy, wild, little kiss that took Dare's breath, and made his arms tighten around her a bit.

"Don't forget me, Allie!"

As if she could! "There ain't been so many folks went out of their way to be good to me," she said tremulously, "that I'm apt to forget! But I'll remember you, Dare—to the end of the road an' back!"

He asked, with fresh, bewildering desolation: "But you ain't comin' back?"

"You forget," she reminded him, with a bitterness he never forgot, "I'm a wagon tramp. Some day, when you least expect it, you'll look down the road an' see the *Santa Maria* rollin' in."

Then, reversing the order of last night, smiling at the last, turning every yard to wave back, taking all the joy out of his dreams, Allie rode away from him.

Suddenly, Corral de Terra was a dead weight on Dare. But he was tied to it—a slave to it—with no hope of escape. He had made the plunge. He had to stay. So unhappily, heavily, he returned to the house.

There he found a six-foot length of animated rawhide smoking on the gallery, and a roan horse making friends with Check.

"Are you the Dare Devil what's resurrectin' this place?" the leathery old-timer inquired.

"I'm Dare *Devlyn*—yes."

"Waal," after a frank and lengthy scrutiny, "I'm Cim."

Dare shook hands on it, too upset about Allie to make talk, or notice the lack of it.

"Do your ears burn?" was the next inquiry. "No?" as Dare denied it. "Waal, they ought to! For you're the most notorious man in the Los Lobos right now. Some folks say you're dead game—saddlin' yourself with this ol' hoodoo. Some say you're a plain fool—an' worse. But one an' all is a-cussin' an' dis-cussin' you to beat six of a kind!"

This was not exactly displeasing to Dare, and he began to take an interest in his venture again.

"Need men?" asked the old puncher, rolling a new cigarette with one hand, and lighting it on the butt of the first one.

"Sure do!" Dare said quickly. "But I'm mighty particular. You see, I'm pickin' 'em for good looks, or bad looks and——"

"I qualify there!"

"Good ridin', or bad reputations——"

"Reckon you didn't catch my name," said the applicant slowly. "I'm Cim—Cimarron White. Was, at one time, foreman for Corral de Terra for the Jessimer boys."

Dare's heart leaped. One of the men he had wondered about. Of all the luck!

"Do you know what kind of a ranch I'm goin' to run?" he asked, almost holding his breath.

"I don't give a hoot! When I heard Corral de Terra was stagin' a come-back, I knowed I couldn't live nohow unless I could ride for the ol' brand ag'in. But I know—Kit told me."

"Well, you can step right into your old job, Cim."

A nod was Dare's thanks. And they sat on in silence, Cim smoking thoughtfully, his eyes bent on the ground, and his boot heel scraping idly.

"I ain't been out—since," he said finally. And Dare knew he meant since that black day that had been the death of the Jessimers. "It all comes back. Joe died right where you set. When I could get—to him——" He choked. Presently he went on: "There was shells ankle deep on this here gallery an' ground——"

Stooping, he picked up a corroded, misshapen bit of metal that his boot had kicked up. "One of Joe's cattridges," he said, and handed it over to Dare. And the boy saw his eyes gleaming fiercely under their heavy, black brows, saw his face strangely work, and tingled to the hate in his curse: "Dang their black hearts!"

He spoke as though it had happened but yesterday. And it was, in fact, more real than yesterday's happenings to Cim, except such of yesterday's happenings as were a far echo of it. The report, for instance, that Cull Cole was inviting all Los Lobos sheepmen to join him in taking the range north of Rio.

"An' if—*when*—that happens," Cimarron White told Dare, "you'll see the ol' days of the Lobos reenacted right here!"

But things were so quiet, Dare could not believe it, and with all his old vim he set to work, directing his army of men, under the eyes of the Los Lobos Range. For, as Cim had said, every one had sat up and taken notice of him. Never a day but curious ranchers rode in to watch his progress, poke sly fun at his venture, or mutter dark prophecies. Fierce-eyed old-timers watched the rebuilding of Corral de Terra in silence, fiercely rejoiced in it—for it clinched the cattlemen's claim on the range north of the Upper Rio beyond dispute.

Cull Cole, sheep king of the Los Lobos, was stirred to drastic action by reports of Dare's activities.

"That block is ours by the old truce!" he harangued other sheepmen. "If we want it, men, we've got to take it. Our claim won't hold water once Corral de Terra's herd goes on that range! An' I, for one, don't aim to be euchred out of it!"

Terrible forces were sweeping the Los Lobos Range, and Dare Devlyn was only a chip in the raging stream! But he worked happily, envisioning the day when he would have everything going, and a houseful of folks to supply with excitement.

And many times each day, he looked out over the court—blued with the lupines that always evoked for him the sad, sweet, gypsyish face of Allie Boone—in the vain hope of seeing the *Santa Maria* roll in.

CHAPTER VI

A FINE JOB

THE Corral de Terra had come to life again, reassumed its position of proud importance in the wide Los Lobos Range. Again, all attention was centered on it, again, the least thing that went on there was of tremendous interest and influence. And it bore in its resurrection little resemblance to the melancholy ruin it had been. Still old, but beautiful, with the grand, austere inimitable beauty of age.

Heavy doors, in keeping with the architecture, hung in place. The high-arched, Spanish windows sparkled with new glass. A new foundation had taken the sag out of the gallery, and the whole aspect of the structure was changed. Vines still climbed the gray walls, still clung to the chimney of the great fireplace wherein now leaped flames that eagerly consumed the dank chill and musty smell of the rooms. But the tripping, entangling vines in the court were gone.

Weeds had been cleared from the grounds, and water splashed in the ditches again. Once more barns and buildings stood sturdy and strong, and the flowered earth of the rebuilt corrals was again hard-packed by milling hoofs. Herds peacefully grazed on the slopes that lifted to the wild Nimbres, and over all, and of all unchanged and changeless, towered El Capitan.

Seeing all this, as he drove out in his buckboard to consult Dare on a matter entirely apart from his regular line, Kit Kress was amazed. And when he stopped the rig at the gate in the wall, to watch men busy at various tasks, horses stamping and snorting in the corrals, and cattle on the slopes, it was so like the Corral de Terra of old that, in the strange mood engendered by something that had happened this day, his mind played tricks, and this scene faded from his eyes. It was replaced by one that made his sluggish old blood leap like the young blood that had once run like wine in his veins, and his old heart pound like the mad thing that had functioned in youth.

It was night, and the range beat to the thunder of galloping hoofs, as dark riders swept past, crying: *"Ride, Lobos!"* under trusted windows as they went. And men tumbled from bunks to saddle. Plunging, clashing, crashing horses filled the night. Red flame stabbed the dark. Screams, shots, oaths—swallowed up in a mighty roar. Ride, spur, curse—*Ride, Lobos!* An arm thrown up in the dark. Red fire again. A cry, smothered by something more potent than noise. Another dark mass on the ground, another stark face staring up from the grass, another empty saddle hurtling past. And a running stirrup touching his——

"All right, Kit?"

"All right, Lynne!"

Then to wake, having felt that! To wake in a *buckboard!* Never again to ride widely, wildly, as he had ridden then! And to be *glad* of it, to pray there would never be need of it, and to tremble in fear that there would!

The cowboy who had opened the gate stared hard as Kress drove by him with never a sign. "Breakin' fast," he told the first waddy he met. "Well, Kit's old!" was the matter-of-fact response.

Old, yes—like the old house, but still young enough to appreciate the humor of what he saw, driving up to the barn—gaudy, gunned punchers, sheepishly returning his grin, knowing, as Kit did, that, had Corral de Terra been what it was, instead of a show place, they would be laughed off the range. And when a long, brown, wrinkled, old puncher, in a pink shirt, yellow bandanna, villainous six-guns that sagged his holsters, and a half-acre hat, stepped out of the barn and tried to slink past, Kit roared outright:

"Cim! Why, you ol' bird of paradise! An' at *your* age!"

Cimarron White—foreman of Corral de Terra now, as in the stirring times Kit well remembered— turned red as a beet.

"Willie's all dressed up fer comp'ny," he said sheepishly. "I can't play with you, Kit. Might muss my ha'r, or muddy my pretties."

Kit's mirth vanished. "The first lot's due then?" he asked.

"On to-day's train," Cim said soberly. "To-day we're reactin' the ol' days fer the dudes—or the young idea of ol' days. It's bad business, Kit!"

"How, Cim?"

Cim's voice dropped. "Kit, Dare's staged a sham battle to amuse them thrill eaters! Hired Lars Hansen to drive his sheep over the slope up there— where the crowd can see from the gallery. He's goin' to tell 'em the sheep's invadin' our range, an' our boys are shootin' it out with them. Guns, of course, to be loaded with blanks. It's a lark, Kit— but right now it's bad business to dig up ol' memories like that! I've talked till I'm black in the face, but it goes in one ear, an' out the other. He thinks I'm an old fogy, Kit."

Gravely they stared at each other.

"Kit"—Cim hunched over the wheel—"you know Cull's crowdin' his sheep up on the Rio? You know the cowmen's just waitin' for———"

"I know! I'm as worried as—— Here comes your boss, Cim."

Guiltily, the old foreman withdrew as Dare came up, genuinely glad to see Kit.

"Cim tells me," said the agent, as they shook hands, "that the curtains' about due to go up."

"The minit the train pulls into Sundown." Dare's dark eyes danced with fun.

"Well," Kit smiled back, "first impressions are most lastin', folks say."

"I sure aim theirs to be!" Dare put his boot on the hub of Kit's wheel, and looked up at him with a small-boy grin. "We took all the springs out of the ol' Bain wagon that we're bringin' 'em out in, an' I've hired ten of the wildest-lookin' characters I could scare up in the county to escort 'em out—ky-yi-in' every step an' shootin' blanks. An' we ain't fetchin' 'em out the regular road by a long shot, but up that ol' mine road over the Hump. If there's a worse one in these parts, I've yet to find it, an' I've scouted some!"

"The rocky road to Dublin ain't in it!" laughed Kress.

"Cim's drivin' 'em out, an' he's got his instructions

to give 'em an appetite for—— Gee, I'm a great
one! Git out, Kit—dinner's still on the table."

"Thanks, son—but I et."

Dare rumpled his dark hair, smiling ruefully.
"Reckon it's just as well, for I rather overplayed
my hand when it came to a cook. You see, half
the letters I got asked did we have Spanish *cuisine*"
—which was not the way Dare pronounced it—"an' I
wrote back that we did. So I hired Josefa—Pedro's
mother-in-law—to cook, so I could make good. Ever
since, we've went around with our tongues hangin'
out. She sprinkles food on the pepper, Kit! Tamales,
chili—— For Pete's sake, why do they call it
'chilly'?"

Kit said it was too deep for him.

"Well, get out, Kit. I want to show you what
I've done."

With the agent limping beside him, Dare toured the
ranch. And Kress marveled at the change the boy
had wrought. It seemed incredible that it could have
been accomplished in a month, and proved what the
vision and fire of youth could do, when backed by
capital, credit, and brains. He said, in all sincerity:

"A fine job, son!"

"Outside," specified Dare moodily. "But something's wrong with the house. Oh, it's full of chairs,
beds, tables, an' things—but it looks like a barn."

"What you need," advised Kit, searching his mind
for a person to fit, "is a nice, homy ol' woman to fix
things up."

"A *young* woman," corrected the boy, his moody
gaze on the lupines. "One so young, you couldn't
hardly call her a woman yet. Little, but oh my!
You know, *that* kind."

Kress glanced at him curiously. "You've some one in mind," he said.

The boy sighed. "All the time!"

They stopped under the sycamores, and Kress looked away from Dare and up at El Capitan, frowning down.

"Son, is it true you've staged a sham battle tonight?"

"Sure is!" Laughter welled up in Dare's eyes again. Kit hadn't realized he was so young.

"I wouldn't," the old man said, and laid both hands on Dare's arm. Anxiety sharpened his tone. "I wouldn't do it, son."

The boy shrugged impatiently. "Still harpin' on danger, Kit? I've give up all hope of it, myself! This country's dead—deader'n the Pecos, an' it should 'a' been buried years back. Holy cow, I'm just fakin' excitement! I can't see any danger in that. I can't see any chance for danger in *anything* around this here place!"

"There's always danger when the interests of one group of men clash with those of another—when differences are settled with guns. But there's more to this, son. The ol' feud's *livin'*, I tell you! It will take the best efforts of every sane citizen to hold it down. If there's one outbreak—*one*—the fat's in the fire! If Gid Perkins locks horns with Cull Cole——"

"Kit, you're loco on that subject!" Dare was amused. "I've met Gid an' I've seen Cull Cole, an' they're the peaceablest, harmlessest ol' codgers I ever seen! I can't feature them lockin' horns or their doin' any damage to speak of, if they did."

Kit was very serious now. "Call a halt on that battle, son."

Dare was impressed, but he had gone too far to retract.

"I can't." He was honest about it. "I promised excitement. I'd be takin' money under false pretenses—be a cheat—if I didn't come through."

"At the cost of bloodshed?" cried Kress. "To thrill a pack of dudes, you'd kill——"

"No," Dare said soberly. "Not if I knew that would happen. But I don't. Neither do you. I don't even believe it, Kit. So I've no excuse not to go on. Listen." He pulled a sheaf of letters and telegrams out of his pocket, squatted on his heels, and smoothed them out on his knee.

"This one"—lifting the first—"is from a rich young buck—Jasper Kade, he calls hisself—back in Buffalo. Listen, Kit:

"Your promise to give me a thrill is a challenge I'm taking. So far I've found life a bore. Book me from the 15th, indefinitely. Check inclosed.

"There's a lot of 'em, Kit," said Dare, his dark face glowing with earnestness, "an' they all crave one thing—excitement with a capital E! Women's as crazy for it as men. Here's one from a woman—a New Hampshire schoolma'am, Eloise Hays. I've had a bunch of letters from her. Poor girl, she ain't been out of a schoolroom for years. Smell it, Kit."

"Phew!" Kress made a face as that missive was wafted under his nose. "Violets, an' violet ink! Son, watch out for that dame!"

Dare blushed. "It's what it *says,*" he explained stiffly, "not how it smells, that gits under my skin." And he read:

"Pencils, paper, chalk, an 'Please, teacher, can I do this or do that?' until I'm going mad! Dare Devlyn, give me a breath of free, pure air; give me the stars to spread like a canopy over me, and mountains fresh from the hand of God! Give me adventure! Then, if some swash-buckling cowboy slings me over his saddle and bears me off to his lair——"

"Lair?" Kit's eyebrows shot up interrogatively.
"Den," Dare explained. "She thinks we're wild, Kit." He concluded the rhapsody:

"——I'd die happy. But, oh, don't let me die until I have lived!"

Visibly affected, Dare refolded the letters, returned them to his pocket, and stood beside Kit, who was eying him in a way that made him color to the roots of his hair.

"Um-m-m," mused the agent, "I begin to see there's dangers in this scheme of yours that I didn't suspect."

Dare dug the toe of his boot into the ground and kept his eyes on it. He had romanced a bit about Eloise, pictured her just a slim, big-eyed, little thing as Allie Boone, unhappy because she was missing the best part of life. Well, she'd be having it soon. He looked at his watch—three hours yet. Not much time in which to rehearse the million things he had to, if everything was to go off smoothly. He could give Eloise the free air, put a star canopy over her, but adventure—he'd have to make that.

"That," he told Kress, with finality, "is why I can't half my fake battle. Here's how I figger: These ol' fellows has had their fling. If they git in the way of the band wagon, it's up to them; but it ain't right, Kit, to checkrein young folks on their account. Listen: A hombre gits throwed by a horse—does that stop ridin'? A puncher gits gored in a round-up—does that stop round-ups, even the one where it happened at? No! An' when I think of the school-teacher, praying to be relieved, for a while at least, from the dreary monotonous life of a little New England village—praying not to be let die till she's lived—why, I know I'm right, Kit. Those people who have passed all their lives in the crowded cities have never known what real living is. I can show 'em the time of their lives! Mebbe, after all, that's what I was born for."

Too wise to waste words on a young zealot with a noble purpose in life, Kit gave in. Possibly he *was* touched on the subject, he told himself. After all, it was a joke, and he had no reason to think that Los Lobos folks lacked a sense of humor, so he got down to the business that had brought him here.

"Got room for two more boarders, son?"

"Just," rejoined Dare. "I'll have a full house then. Who wants to come?"

"A—a—man," Kit faltered. "A—a ol' friend of mine—Jim Grant, an' his girl, Madge. They're from Maine. But they're in town now an' want to come out to-morrow some time."

"Send 'em out to-night with the bunch," Dare grinned. "Let 'em git in on the excitement, Kit!"

A queer smile crossed the still features of Kress. "Excitement?" he slowly repeated. "No, Dare, I don't think this man will be interested in your excitement."

CHAPTER VII

THE DUDES ARRIVE

ALL Sundown was at the depot to meet the west-bound train and see Corral de Terra's guests arrive, and to regale the brief wait by joshing Dare's crew, whose loud scarfs, shirts, chaps, and artillery made them conspicuous targets for good-natured gibes. None of which the dude wranglers minded a bit—with this huge time in prospect on the old ranch to-night! And they gave back as good as was sent —with the exception of their foreman, Cimarron White.

Cim, though gorgeous as any, took no part in the fun, but paced the platform, solemn and silent, his mouth set in a grim, hard line. He had had his say. All he could do was to stand by and help pick up the pieces when these heedless young fools were through.

And Dare Devlyn—a snappy figure again, in the glittering raiment he had worn into the Los Lobos Range—was as solemn as Cim. Now that the curtain was about to go up, he was on needles and pins. Dare realized all of a sudden the chance he was taking. He had staked every cent of his ten thousand dollars on this wild throw. If he failed, he was a lot worse than busted, and every one predicted that he would fail. Every one had discouraged him from the start, made fun of him, called him a thrill-rancher," a "hair-raiser," and worse. He wanted to make good to show them. He *had* to make good!

The setting seemed perfect to him—these big, empty plains all around, the black, jagged mountains beyond, this genuine old cow town, the "natives" here, the remuda of cow ponies stamping up dust and trailing their reins, and the four-horse team of half-broken buckskins hitched to the springless old Bain wagon that was to take the folks out. Yes, it ought to go over big. He could not think of a thing he had overlooked. Now, if the last act of the exciting reception he had planned for Eloise—for all the crowd—came off as scheduled——

Nervous about that at the last moment, he corralled his crew, each one of whom seemed to him perfect for the rôle he would play.

"Boys," said Dare, "let's be dead sure we've got everything straight. The idea is not to give them a moment to think of themselves till they turn in to-night. There's not a chance of that going out, and the boys at the ranch are waitin' to relay it on. But the fight—we can't risk a slip-up there, so let's go over that.

"Now, while the folks are at supper, Las Vegas comes in an' asks me for orders. I tell him to take the crew an' stand guard to-night, to shoot any sheepman he catches invadin' our range. See? All of you—but Cim, here, an' me—hide in them rocks below the ridge, where I showed you. Then, when Lars an' his men come over the right——" Dare broke off and, singling out an extremely picturesque puncher said, "Las Vegas, did you send them blank cartridges up to the sheep camp?"

Blithely, Las Vegas affirmed that he had.

"Well," continued Dare, steadfastly avoiding the glum, foreboding face of old Cim, "when Lars'

sheep shows up over on the ridge—at seven sharp—
I'll have the crowd out on the gallery. We see the
sheep comin'. We see you-all a-gallopin' for 'em,
shootin' off blanks. I yell to Cim that we gotta
massacre 'em, an' him an' me jumps on our horses an'
rides to the fracas. Keep bangin' away! Remember, the dudes are watchin', an' they don't know
it's blanks, don't know it's faked! Stampede the
sheep back over the ridge, but keep up the shootin' till
you're plumb outta earshot. Now—got that?"

"Yeah," a happy chorus assured him, "down pat."

Dare relaxed. "If that don't give 'em a thrill,
nothin' will! Of course, they're bound to know later
that it was a frame-up, same as they'll know there
was a regular road we could 'a' took 'em out over——
By the way, Cim, did you have plenty of rocks piled
on that hill road?"

"Where thar was room for 'em." Cim came
mighty near smiling then.

"Well, keep the team steppin'——"

"Here comes the train!"

The crew scurried to position. The curious crowd
surged toward the singing rails. The train whistled,
and clanged, and snorted in. And Dare leaped on
Check and circled the depot at a furious pace, his
maneuver timed with such precision that he came
tearing down the platform, rudely scattering the in-
nocent bystanders, just as the last passenger alighted
from the Pullman. And, lifting his sombrero high,
he pulled his paint pony to a spectacular halt, right in
the astonished faces of his tenderfoot guests.

Leaping down, his eyes eagerly sought a slim,
little thing who had not been out of a schoolroom for
years. But he failed to see her that instant, and was,

in the next, overwhelmed by the visitors—so confounded by the babble of tongues, explanations, questions, introductions, that his welcoming speech fled from his mind and he just stood still, taking the shocks as they came.

A woman—fair, fat, and forty—had both his hands. Her baby-blue eyes had a baby-doll stare, her face—pink and white as a baby's—was framed by curls the color of corn silk, and a bright, tight, little red hat, and she smelled like certain of the letters Dare had received—like a whole acre of violets after a rain! She exclaimed in a babyish gurgle: "Oh, Mr. Devlyn, this *heavenly* air—so pure and free! O-oh, I can feel it clear to my toes!"

But even before she had uttered a word, the bubble of romance had burst with a bang. Eloise! Dare had time for but one fleeting thought—that it would take a whole canopy of stars to cover Eloise—before she was jostled aside by a rubicund, middle-aged man, in a plaid cap and plus fours, who lugged a golf bag that was loaded for bear, and whose first words were: "Are we close to the links?" Even as he spoke, he had one of the clubs out of the bag and was waggling it with the dangerous vim that came of having been confined for five days on the train.

Deftly ducking the swing, Dare politely regretted that they were not, but that——

"There's always a golf course handy," interjected the enthusiast.

And when Dare said, "Not here, there ain't— handy or otherwise," Ezra Biggers wailed apologetically: "But how'll I get my exercise?"

Assuring him that they would try to supply it,

Dare found himself being given the once over by Mrs. Abraham Mills of Schenectady—a spare, meticulous person, who seemed made up of concentrated dignity rather than mere flesh and blood, and who was the last person one would ever suspect of harboring a vulgar relish for thrills. Yet Dare recalled that she was the society dame, who did not want the range trouble settled before she got here. He was wondering, flashingly, how she could look like that, groomed to a hair, like she'd just stepped out of a bandbox, when a dark, anæmic young man, in a Palm Beach suit and with patent-leather hair, waved him a limp hand, saying feebly:

"I'm sorry I came on the opening day. It always means a crush, and crushes bore me. I've been so bored with the trip, I'm sunk. And all I've seen of this country bores me far more."

Jasper Kade! The rich young buck from Buffalo who had challenged Dare to give him a thrill, because he was so bored with life. But not as bored, Dare bet, as he was with Jasper already!

Then Dare got fleeting impressions of a sensible girl in horn-rimmed spectacles, of her mother and brother, bespectacled and sensible, too; of the Hiltons, a pair of icebergs, whom he despaired of ever being able to melt; of the infantile Eloise in raptures over his paint pony——

"Doesn't he look like a ze-bra! Oh, Mr. Devlyn, do say he's a cayuse! I'm mad about cayuses! I must have a picture of myself riding him to send back to my poppa!"

Dare would not insult Check by calling him a cayuse to please her. And he had a picture of her riding his horse! Then he had another of himself and Eloise, leading the procession through a grinning lane of townsmen to where his own crew waited—with grins. And he found, to his utter surprise and mortification, a beribboned box of chocolate creams, a kodak, and a flame-silk umbrella in his hands, with no idea on earth how they came to be there!

Then they came to the wagon. The buckskins were train shy, and it was all the four cowboys, hanging to their ears, could manage to hold them down. The sensible mother logically demanded assurance of Dare that the horses were safe.

"Why, of course they're safe!" sweetly Eloise answered for him. "I'm sure we can trust Mr. Devlyn."

Dare felt like hunting for a hole and crawling into it, when he saw Cim's face—wreathed with its first real grin that day.

Now, in the bustle of loading the wagon, it somehow came to pass that Dare had to lift Eloise in. And he was ungallant enough to wonder how the most swashbucklin' buckaroo could sling her over a saddle—say he was loco and wanted to! But at last all the dudes were snug on the blankets and buffalo robes, spread none too thick on the wagon bed, and Cim, high on the driver's seat, gathered the reins. The armed and leather-lunged escore had mounted.

"Ready?" yelled Cim.

And Dare gayly signaled, "Let 'em buck!"

With an elegant flourish, Cim's lash snapped like a pistol shot over the backs of the mettlesome buckskins. Wildly they lunged ahead, precipitating the passengers as suddenly back. And to the whoops and shots of their wild-looking escort and their own star-

tled shrieks—shrillest of which rang those of the irrepressible Eloise—the party was off in a cloud of
dust.

Through town they dashed at a headlong gallop,
and streaked over the plains. Now with the riders
shooting and shouting about the wagon; now, as
Cim gave the buckskins their heads, hidden from it
by the dust pouring out behind.

"Cim's got the spirit!" Las Vegas yelled at one of
these times.

"I knew he would when we got goin'!" exulted
his youthful boss.

And Cim had the spirit so strongly that they did
not overtake him again in the five miles to the road
forks, where he slowed down to give the team a
chance to recover its wind before taking the branch
road over the Hump. Dare, crowding Check alongside the wagon, found himself beside Eloise.

"Isn't this thr-rilling!" she gasped. "But why do
you do it—shoot, I mean, and yell like that?"

"Bandits!" explained the boy tersely. "These hills
are alive with 'em. If they didn't know there was
men along with the wagon, they might carry you off
for ransom, or"—he paused darkly—"worse!"

Instead of the shrill squeal of terror he had anticipated when he thought of that line, Eloise smiled
up at him like a trustful child.

"Oh, but *you* would rescue me! I wouldn't mind."

Just then, luckily for Dare, the wagon swung into
the mountain road, where Cim had made two rocks
grow where nature had planted but one. The buckskins took it like birds, skimming up the steep grade,
with the wagon coming after them *rattlety-bang!*
This frightened the animals to a more desperate pace,

and if they did not actually run away, they were near enough to it to thrill even a person in on the joke.

The trail wound itself around the shelf of a wall, a series of hairpin curves, and was so narrow that it took a driver of Cim's caliber to render it safe, so narrow that the passengers could look into the dark abyss that dropped off to the left—had they remained in one position long enough to look. But, mercifully, they caught only brief, appalling glimpses of it as they bounced up or came down, and the riders, crowded back here, missing none of the spectacle, were doubled over their saddles in the effort to hide their laughs.

For as Cim whipped up, *bumpity-bump,* the sensible girl and her sensible kin, all but lost in the shuffle, worked their legs over the end gate, ready to jump in a crisis. Jasper Kade clutched everything clutchable, in a new and violent interest in life. The dignity was all jolted out of Mrs. Mills and, with hat and hair awry, she looked almost human. Ezra Biggers, the disappointed golfer, reduced to shorter pants than ever, was climbing, hand over hand, by the edge of the wagon box—which his look plainly said he feared might be the Golden Stair—up to the driver's seat and Cim.

"Stop!" he pleaded, his eyes as round as his golf balls, and as big. "If you can't stop—please slow up! Please! Please!"

"Can't!" Cim flung back. "They'd go over the grade! Momentum's what's keepin' us on! If we lose momentum, we're gone!"

"Good scout, Cim!" Dare applauded to the rest. "He thought *that* up all by hisself!"

Just then the shock of surmounting an extra big boulder jounced Ezra back into Mrs. Mills' arms— to the unholy glee of the saddle brigade.

But the wagon was over the worst, and the foaming buckskins now raced down the slope, streaked out on the regular highway, skimmed along the high adobe wall of Corral de Terra, through the gate which unseen hands swung open for them, and came to a dead halt in the court.

As cowboys sprang to the heads of the quivering team, and the passengers strove to reassemble their parts, there was an ear-splitting yell from the nearest corral:

"Whoop-e-e-e!"

A bawling, red-eyed outlaw—which Dare had bought from a traveling rodeo—bucked out of the gate, twisting, back-jumping, sunfishing with such insane fury that the boys forgot the act was staged and whooped it up for Pete's sake.

"Ride 'im, Mace!" they cried.

The fascinated visitors watched this exhibition of broncho-busting with gasps of horror that changed into screams as the frenzied outlaw bucked straight for the wagon and seemed, horribly, to rear over it.

Then Las Vegas, cast for the hero's part, sent his horse between and wildly shouting, waving his hat, hazed the outlaw—none knew where. For they had barely scrambled from the wagon when Eloise— who had needed no help from Dare in getting out— pointed the flame-colored parasol, and suddenly helplessly screamed:

"A bull! A mad bull! And I've got red on!"

The paralyzed wagoners saw a wicked-looking but really dog-gentle, long-horned Texas steer seemingly charging for them, but actually herded their way by Sam, who, galloping alongside, leaped from his horse to the longhorn and brought the steer crashing to earth not ten feet from the wagon.

But the bulldogging part of the program was a dead loss, for the audience was in wild stampede for the house.

Josefa—fat, brown, old Josefa, Dare's housekeeper and cook—stationed on the gallery to do the honors for Corral de Terra, took one look at the scared and panicky mob coming her way and, throwing her apron over her face, waddled within, every one of her two hundred pounds quaking with helpless laughter.

Dare, bringing up the rear, all but helpless himself, prayed that the final act would go over as big.

But faint and far, from over the Nimbres, came the rumble of thunder, as though even the voice of nature was lifted in a last warning for hot-headed, hot-blooded youth to go slow!

CHAPTER VIII

OLD DUST

THE crowd was given only a brief respite in which to remove the dust of travel, and no time whatever to think of themselves. Then they sat down to dinner in the high-ceilinged dining room, over which the deep-embrasured, stained-glass windows cast a dim, religious light. Formality had been lost on the mountain road, dignity likewise, and having shared many novel and exhilarating experiences in common, the guests discussed their survival with the unreserve of old friends. All were enraptured with the historic old house—with the exception of Jasper Kade, who had recovered his languor and was as markedly bored as before, and the hopelessly frozen Hiltons.

It was well that this mood prevailed, for Dare was proving an indifferent host. He sat at the head of the table, but his mind was on the sham battle to follow—the grand climax to their reception. One interest only he had in the meal. He had given Josefa permission to pepper away, and one taste of the food on his plate was painful proof that she had taken full advantage of it. And he was curious to know how these people, who had asked for it, could possibly get away with the Spanish *cuisine*. But he got a new respect for their ability to take punishment, as they ate, with only a politely repressed cough or two, and the unobtrusive assistance of water. Probably they were used to it.

Everything was going smoothly, and the meal was at its height, when, true to schedule, the hoofs of a dozen riders rang in the court, and Las Vegas stalked in.

"Orders, boss?"

Politely excusing himself to his guests, Dare turned in his chair, with a careful avoidance of Las Vegas' eye lest it be fatal to both.

"Ride that west fence!" he snapped. "See that no man bats an eye till crack o' dawn!" He was proud of that—"crack o' dawn." Sounded a heap more to the point than "morning." "Shoot the first mutton-walker that pokes his nose—or a sheep—over that ridge!"

The clatter of forks was strangely hushed.

Grimly, as he got a strangle hold on a laugh, Las Vegas nodded and asked:

"Shoot high, boss, or—straight?"

"Straight!"

On that grim cue, the punched stalked out. Dear silence followed his exit. The gallop of retreating horsemen beat into the room and died. Nonchalantly, Dare ate on, then, finally pretending to notice that he was eating alone, and to be surprised at their horrified stares, he said with a smile of apology:

"Sorry, folks, but we're apt to have a little trouble to-night. Nothin' serious. Just a small difference to be adjusted. There's a locoed sheepman tryin' to jump my range. I aim to show him his place. But it's nothin'—nothin' that need disturb you in the least."

"Do I understand," faltered Ezra Biggers, his

face less ruddy than usual, "that you gave orders to *kill* a person merely for trespass?"

"Depends on your definition of 'person,'" said Dare, in a way that made them all gasp. Ezra turned actually pale.

"But, my dear fellow," he expostulated, "the law——"

"Out here," said Dare, with dark significance, "we make our own law!" Gee, that was a knock-out sure! he reflected.

"But surely, Mr. Devlyn"—Eloise was inspired by a thought truly sublime—"surely in these great, big, wide-open spaces"—indicating their size by the spread of her arms—"there is room for *all* of God's creatures?"

"Which," said the boy tersely, "eliminates sheep! No range is roomy enough for me an' a sheepman. Savvy? I've rattled warnin's aplenty. This time, *I strike!*"

They jumped as though he *had* struck them! Dare decided he had sure missed his calling—ought to be on the stage.

They left the table soon after. The Hiltons coldly retired at once to their room. But Dare did not even have to use the ruse he had invented to get the rest out on the gallery. They drifted there naturally. And, despite the strain they labored under, the view held them enthralled.

Never had the Los Lobos been so beautiful, never so wild and lonely, never so expressive of the sad and ominous spirit that brooded over the range. Dark clouds, massed at intervals in the almost limitless expanse of sky, gave the grand sweep of mountain and plain a theatrical effect of shadow and

light, color and change. Out of the clouds thunder
rolled intermittently. The air was electric. Sunset
fired the towering crags on the left with its exquisite
hues of violet, red, and gold, and awesome and aloof,
El Capitan soared high over them.

"It makes me nervous," twittered Eloise, sidling
up to Dare. "I feel as though it was going to fall
down on me!"

He assured her that the old mountain would stand
up for a few years more, and then, to keep her and
the rest out there and still on edge for the few moments remaining till seven, he recounted the tragic
story of Corral de Terra, wishing that Swap were
here to tell it, and make these dudes feel as he had
felt on hearing it in the fire glow of the river
camp.

"Men call it Hell's Pocket." He dropped his voice
a note or two, copying Swap's deep tone and words
as closely as he could. "They say the curse of God
is on it. Two score of saddles was emptied forever,
in the big fight within these walls!"

He had a qualm of conscience as the nervousness
of his listeners became more apparent. And, as the
moments crept to seven, he could hardly keep his
own attention from straying; his eyes wandered from
the ridge up there where the sheep were to appear
to the rocks below, where Las Vegas and the boys
were hiding. And he was peeved at Cim, "the old
crab," for not lending a tongue to help him out.
But Cim, blind to the appealing glances Dare cast
his way, smoked on in the shade of a pillar, his gaze
on the distant range, and his thoughts years back.

At last, unable to invent further, Dare looked at
his watch. Seven o'clock! The hour when the cur-

tain should rise on the last act. He looked up at the ridge. There was no sign of a sheep on its brow. And, summarily leaving his audience, he walked to the west end of the gallery for a better view. He couldn't understand this delay. He had warned Lars to be on the dot!

"Son"—Dare swung impatiently to see that Cim had followed him up—"it ain't too late to call a halt. I could ride up there, an'——"

"Oh, for Pete's sake, Sim!"

"Dare"—the old foreman's tone and expression were the same Kit Kress had used to him—"it's just play fer you—a game. But it's a dangerous game, one that plenty of folks hereabouts has played in grim earnest! It might set 'em thinkin'. Son, it's too much like the real thing to be——"

Resentfully, the boy walked away. These old fellows who had had their fun did not want young folks even to play at fighting! Call the show off? Not much! Why, if this part fizzled, the whole thing would fall flat. He had to keep the crowd keyed up to the right pitch, too.

So he went back and showed them the marks of lead in the casings, the spot where Joe and Pete Jessimer had been killed, and where Lynne had been found, "holdin' the fort alone, pumpin' lead from two six-guns so hot that they fired the grass when he fell, with a dozen bullet holes in him!" And he told them how Lynne, at the head of the Lobos, had avenged his brothers and fled, no one knew where, but when, "as with sad frequency happens in these wild Nimbres, some hombre runs onto a rusted ol' firin' piece in the grass an' the skull of a human, he thinks hard of the last Jessimer—Lynne!" And all the time Dare talked, his gaze kept straying up there to the ridge above, and his nervousness mounted.

He could see the bright blurs that were the shirts of his riders. They had come out from behind the rocks to hold a powwow, nervous at this delay themselves.

The guests watched Dare's every move. Strung to high tension by his ruthless order to Las Vegas, by the stories he had told them of past strife, by the feeling of tragedy in the very air of Corral de Terra, they wanted to remonstrate with their host, but refrained from some fantastic fear that he, or that forbidding old foreman of his, might order them shot at sunrise as sheep sympathizers.

Even the aristocratic, white-haired Mrs. Mills allowed her feelings to show in a shiver that set all the bright sequins on her smart dinner gown quivering.

"Why should any one desire excitement?" she asked tremulously. "After all, peace——"

" 'He jests at scars that never felt a wound'!" nervously quoted Ezra Biggers.

"So far, I haven't seen anything to get excited about!" put in Jasper Kade, with an animation that showed he was jumpy himself.

Hortense, the sensible girl, and her mother and brother, made no comment. Dare saw the veiled smile they exchanged, and knew they were not fooled. His heart warmed to them for being good sports—not giving away the joke.

Seven fifteen! Almost beside himself, Dare walked to the far end of the gallery again, and Eloise timidly pursued him, her heart interest in the handsome cowboy superseded by one purely professional.

For, as a school-teacher, she was trained in the handling of incorrigible youth.

"I find the Western views so different," timidly, she opened the lesson.

"They would be!" Impatiently, Dare scanned the one before him, still seeing no sheep on it.

"The mental outlook, I mean, the way you look at things. Poppa says that competition is the life of trade. Poppa has a drug store, but when Mr. Seaton came into his district and set up in the same business, poppa didn't shoot Mr. Seaton."

"No?" Dare affected surprise at such tolerance.

"No, he just tried to sell better goods, to compete with him in such a way that——"

"You can't compete with a sheepman." Dare wished she would leave him alone. "Plant one, an' he'll overrun the country. Now an' then, you gotta thin 'em out."

"But nothing, Mr. Devlyn, is so important as human life!"

"Range is a blamed sight more——" Dare's heart bounded with joy, for the sheep were coming at last. Not over the ridge he had expected, though, but across the draw from it, a quarter mile south. That was funny! He had taken Lars up there and showed him the spot. But trust a wool-witted sheep-herder to ball things up if he could! Well, it didn't matter what ridge, so long as they came.

And they were coming, hundreds of them! He had not had any idea that Lars' band was so big. Gee, it was pretty—Dare grudgingly thought—all those white sheep tumbling down the dark slope, like a waterfall! It occurred to him as strange that none of the folks exclaimed at this—to them—sure sign of war. Glancing around, Dare saw that they were not looking at the sheep, but, with unconcealed apprehension, at himself!

Suppressing a grin, he looked back up the slope, and his fear that his men would not see the sheep on that opposite ridge was dispelled as they mounted and wildly galloped across the draw, their shrill whoop beating down on the court, bringing the tense group that way.

"Sheep!" Dare's delight curdled their blood. "Every man out. We'll plumb massacre 'em! We'll show 'em! *Cim!*"

Leaving the visitors transfixed with horror by what they thought they were seeing, Dare dashed to the barn. Cim, who had not waited for the order, was already in the saddle and away. Only Check's superior fleetness enabled Dare to catch up. On they galloped, while up there on the ridge the punchers circled the first of the flock, whooping it up like Comanches, the *bang-bang* of their blanks resounding with machine-gun rapidity. Everything was going off fine!

Conscious of the tense eyes watching below, Dare spurred hard. He could not have ridden more recklessly had the farce been real. It sure looked real, even to him. Up there a man dropped from the saddle—real as life! In fact, he feared it was a bit too real—overdrawn. Now a galloping horse pitched headlong, and its rider rolled over and over, regained his feet, and ran like a deer for the nearest rock. Something cold and smothery came over Dare.

"Cim," he jerked huskily, over the thud of their hoofs, "that horse—the horses ain't trained!"

"You fool!" Cim cried bitterly, yanking blanks from his gun as he rode and jamming in shells! "You hare-brained fool! Didn't you hear that bullet sing!"

On the ridge, all was confusion. Dare's riders were grouping, gesticulating like madmen, shouting words he could not hear. A cowboy came storming down toward him.

Dare pulled up, crying hoarsely, as Cim plunged on: "Mace, what's wrong?"

"Wrong!" yelled the wildly excited puncher, plowing to a stop. "Wrong? We got the wrong herders! Shot blanks, an' got bullets! Boss, *that was Cull Cole's band!*"

Too stunned to grasp that in all its disastrous import, Dare stared. He was fascinated by something red that seeped through Mace's left sleeve, something that widened, broke through the thick cloth, and trickled down over his beaded gauntlet to the ground. Blood! How? What?

"Mace," he cried, in utter bewilderment, "your arm—you're hurt!"

Dazed, the cowboy looked down at it, seemed to see and to feel it for the first time, nor to think much about it in the greater horror of what he had seen.

"Just nicked," he said swiftly. "But, boss, Las Vegas fell like it was all over with him!"

In a terrible revulsion of feeling, Dare spurred on.

Thunder rolled and rumbled ceaselessly among the crags—Nature's "I told you so!" The vivid play of reflected lightning seemed to show a new seam in the stern face of El Capitan. And the stormy wind picked up the dust that the riders had lifted, bore it high in the air, and sent it whirling, swirling all over the Los Lobos range.

Old Dust—kicked up by a past generation in its own reckless, hot-headed youth and laid by a thirty-year truce—was raised again!

CHAPTER IX

"THIS IS WAR!"

THE wild uproar of shots and shouts had stampeded the sheep. Cull Cole's herders, having fired their deadly volley, were in pursuit of them, and Corral de Terra's crew, left in possession of the ridge, rushed to their fallen men.

Pulling up at the first tense group, with a violence that sat Check back on his haunches, Dare leaped down and crowded through. There on the wind-blown grass, his white, senseless face lifted to the threatening sky, lay Las Vegas. Over him knelt Cim. The old foreman had stripped off his own shirt, and with it was trying to stanch the flow of blood from a ghastly wound just below Las Vegas' right shoulder blade.

And Dare, dropping down beside his puncher, remembering him as he had been a little while ago, so full of life and fun, so eager to help him carry out his joke—his joke—cried thanks to Heaven that Las Vegas lived. He was seriously—dangerously—wounded, but he lived!

It gave Dare strength to rush on and count the awful carnage of this terrible mistake. He rode to where a puncher was propped up against a boulder, his features set in pain, while comrades ripped away his chaps, exposing a long, red furrow plowed by a bullet through the flesh of his leg.

"It's nothin', boss," Sam said jauntily, with a cheerful twist of his lips. "Nothin' that won't come out in the wash."

Bucked up by this game spirit, Dare continued. He passed a horse, injured so badly that it must be shot, and came to where another lay dead, with its prostrate rider motionless in the grass beside it. But even as Dare came up, this fellow got to his feet, and began dazedly feeling himself all over for his injury. He was so surprised to find none that when Dare asked him where he was hit, and waited in dread for the answer, he grinned sheepishly and said:

"Reckon I must 'a' been hit by the hoss."

And that was all! It was enough, but it could have been so much worse that Dare was almost giddy with relief as he rushed back to Las Vegas.

"Bring up a wagon to move him in!" he flung at the cowboys near him. "Sling in a couple of mattresses, an' git back on the double-quick. I've got to follow Cull Cole an' explain!"

There was a strangled, inarticulate cry behind him, and Dare turned to see Cim—a shirtless, disheveled, terrible figure, his fierce eyes flashing like the lightning in the western sky. His leathery face, black as the thundercloud the lightning flashed from, was working in nameless hate—as it had on that day when he had picked up Joe Jessimer's cartridge in the court.

"Explain!" His voice rose to a shrill pitch. "Explain to a sheepman! By Job, *I'm* goin' after Cull, an' there won't be any blanks in my gun! I'm goin' to explain—in the only language that dumb breed savvies. I'll make their mistake in slingin' lead at cowmen plenty plain."

As he lunged by Dare to get his roan, the boy grabbed him. Cim's fury turned on Dare. "Let me go, you yearlin'! Let me go!"

"Why, Cim?" Desperately, Dare maintained his hold. "Why?"

"Why?" cried the old foreman crazily. "Lookit my hands! That's blood on 'em! Blood, spilled by a sheepman! Oh, dang their—— Let me go!"

It took all Dare's strength to hold him, all the phenomenal strength that surged within him to prevent this hideous anticlimax. That strength was born of his new terror at seeing other faces—young faces —taking fire from Cim's!

"Cim, you're loco!" Dare cried sharply. "You're dreamin'! This ain't the old days—wake up. It's a joke, Cim. Funny—if you can see it!" Dare broke into laughter then—grim, senseless laughter that cut through the red haze in Cim's brain, letting a ray of reason in. "Think, Cim, how it looked to Cull—our men bangin' away at him like that! *He* didn't know it was a joke! He didn't know it was blanks! *We* ain't got no call to go on warpath, Cim!"

Cim's face was bewildered—full, still, of the old dream—but he was awake.

"Forgit Cull Cole," he said curtly. "Go down an' git things ready for Las Vegas. I'll wait for the wagon an' come with him."

As Dare mounted and turned Check down the slope, he saw—grimmest joke of all—the sheep they had expected, Lars Hansen's sheep, coming over the appointed ridge! And he saw the herders waiting up

there for the sham attack. But they must have seen
that something was amiss, for one of them—Lars
himself—sent his horse down, meeting Dare in the
draw that lay between, and calling, as he rode up:

"Why don't you shoot?"

Dare's every emotion flared into anger, and he
told Lars why, in no uncertain terms, told him that
Cull Cole had come along and done the shooting,
that, thanks to his delay, three men were crippled—
one might die!

"Gosh, that's bad!" The sheepman whitened, nor
was he thinking of the wounded men. "But it ain't
my fault, Devlyn." Hastily, Lars disclaimed all responsibility. "I started in plenty of time, but I met
a tramp trader down the road a piece, an' swapped
hosses with him. I swapped one of the chuck-wagon
team, an' got done brown, for that slab-sided, wall-
eyed son of a locoed cyclone balked every step of the
way, holdin' us back! If I'd 'a' traded for the knock-
kneed pinto an' the cuckoo clock——"

Too furious to get the significance of that, Dare
tore away to tell the crowd down there what had
happened, to tell them the truth and never more de-
lude them! Excitement! He never wanted to hear
the word again. He had not thought of it much himself since he had bought Corral de Terra; he had
been too busy. Busy folks were not hunting thrills!
These old fellows—Cim and Kit Kress—knew what
they were talking about. They had warned him.
But he had not listened. He had been deaf, dumb, and
blind; he had maybe killed Las Vegas. No use
blaming Lars—any one—it was his own plan.

Sick with remorse, Dare dashed in at the rear
gate of the ranch, just as the wagon rolled out.

Grabbing one of the cowboys, he told him to get the doctor.

"Burn up the road!"

He slid from Check before the barn and was moving toward the house when voices within halted him.

"But, good heavens, man," came Ezra Biggers' voice, exasperated, "this is no time to trade! I tell you, there's a war in progress! Men have been killed!"

"The time to trade," defined a hypnotic voice that rang a bell in Dare's mind, "is when a hombre offers you something you want."

"But I don't want a bootjack! What earthly use have I got for a bootjack?"

"As much as I'll have for these here mallets of yourn!" retorted Swap."

Swap Boone was back—trading Ezra out of his golf clubs! Recalling now what Lars had said, Dare could have laughed at this last, ironic prank of fate. Swap had returned just in time to work off a balky horse on Lars, detaining his outfit, while Cull Cole and his men chanced along—and Cain was raised!

In no mood to greet Swap now, Dare hurried on to prepare his company for the wagon's sad return. Ahead, in the deeper shadows of the sycamores, he saw the *Santa Maria,* and a dozen horses drooping near. A well-remembered little figure stood beside the wheel, and over it bent Jasper Kade, who evidently was not bored now—far from it! Strange that Dare should observe that fact then, when his mind was on the group excitedly awaiting him on the gallery.

But Allie's mind was not on a single thing but Dare. During all that long and lonely month of wan-

dering she had treasured the memory of his wanting
her, his reluctance to let her go. She had carried it
away from Corral de Terra, and she had brought it
back. The glory of that memory was in her eyes
now as she stepped out to meet him—a little diffident
to be seen by these fine folks, but a little prouder of
herself than usual in the red calico dress that she had
made—every stitch of it—herself.

"Dare!" she cried in shy joy, as he neared. Oh,
the pity of it that Allie had not come one short
half hour ago! Then her welcome would have been
all she could desire; for, if it was not love Dare
felt for Allie, it was at least the substance from
which love is made. But now, frantic with remorse,
weighed down by a thousand worries, he had no
time for her. And when he did have time, though
it was only on the morrow—he was hopelessly in love
with some one else!

"Dare!" she called again, thinking he did not see
her.

He paused to take her hand, saying briefly, "Hello,
Allie!" and passed on, leaving her mute, stricken, as
though she, too, had been shot. She had come to
help him. He needed her, he had said. Now, he did
not want her. Why should he want or need her—a
wagon tramp! He would think she had come for
the wages he had promised, the fine clothes——

With no idea of the hurt he had inflicted, Dare
faced his guests, to be confounded, as on his first
meeting with them, by a babble of tongues. Who
had been killed? Who had been hurt? How many
were injured? Petitions for the gory details swamped
him.

"Folks," he began miserably, when there was a

lull in the storm of questions, "that fight you just saw was a joke——"

"*Joke!*" they chorused shrilly.

"Joke!" incredulously soloed Mrs. Mills. "Do you mean to say that you kill men and horses for a joke?"

"Poppa says"—Eloise could understand it—"that the West is a big, strenuous country, and the men it breeds are big in soul and body. He says everything is done on a large scale!"

"Great Scott!" cried Ezra, who had just come up. "What would they do if they were in earnest —if that's the size of their jokes?"

"I mean," Dare blurted desperately, "that I meant it for a joke. I planned to give you a thrill, but——"

"Young man," Mrs. Mills said firmly, "you certainly succeeded. But, mercy goodness, don't go to such lengths to amuse me again!"

Seeing the wagon leaving the ridge, Dare gave up. "They're bringin' in the men," he told them. "Las Vegas is hurt—bad. Will one of you ladies help me, till the doctor gits here?"

Eloise knew she would not! The sight of blood made her faint. Why, once one of her pupils got his head cut open with a baseball bat, and she keeled right——

Hortense thought she might, but when her sensible mother reminded her that she was on vacation, she was level-headed enough to see the point.

Mrs. Mills was sure the hospital was the place for the man, if he were badly hurt. When told that there was no hospital within seventy miles, she was sure there should be—*here,* of all places!

"Rustle clean, white cloths, scissors, soap, water,

an' iodine, Dare," struck in a quiet little voice. "I'll patch 'em up!"

Allie—of course! Flashing her a glance full of gratitude, Dare rushed inside to help Josefa round up the necessaries. Then the women guests, interestedly studying this slip of a girl whose efficiency put them to shame, were one and all possessed of a desire to help. So that all was ready when the wagon was brought to a careful halt before the house, and the injured borne carefully in.

Dark had settled when Dare stepped out on the gallery. He had had a bad quarter of an hour calming other nerves, and his own were jangling. He wanted to be alone here in the cool and quiet, get hold of himself, if he could. He rolled a cigarette, prepared to relax.

"Waal"—a whiskered face poked around the pillar —"how's tricks?"

The answer was too obvious for words, but, even in his disinclination for company, Dare said sincerely: "Glad you're back, Swap! Thought you'd left the country for good."

Swap hooted at the idea. Catch him quitting a prime trading center like that! Nope, he had just pulled out while the ditch-digging preliminaries were being accomplished.

"Swapped off some of them plugs," he confided, "for saddle hosses—guaranteed to be dead easy on a dude. Expect to make a deal with you to-morrow. An' I got a lotta new goods—such as rich folks is most apt to fancy. Yep"—Swap viewed the prospects smugly—"all signs point to a busy season. Wouldn't surprise me none if I swapped the cuckoo off!"

Too nervous to listen to the garrulous trader longer, Dare walked away. Seeing Cim smoking on the bench beneath the sycamore, he drifted toward him.

"Cim," he said brokenly, "I wisht they'd 'a' put me in a sack, along with a good, big rock, an' drowned me afore my eyes were open!"

"Forget it, son."

"I can't! An' if Las Vegas dies, I never can forget. I wanted excitement, Cim, but I overlooked the fact that it usually means heartaches for some one. I envied you-all, Cim, for all the excitement you've been through here. I forgot them that died to make it. I didn't think of the heartaches left with you—rememberin' them that died. An', Cim, when I think of the consequences——"

"You can't!" somberly Cim cut in. "Son, you can't even guess what they'll be! Lord only knows the consequences of——" His head lifted, his long form drew taut in the attitude of listening.

"Hark!" His hand closed like a vise over Dare's arm, and his face was grayer than the gloom should make it.

"Ain't that far shootin', son?"

Dare listened intently, but he heard nothing but the muttering of the storm that had threatened the Los Lobos range and passed around. "No," he said, "it's far thunder, Cim." Nevertheless, dread that he could not define welled up within him, and he added: "Cim, I'd best hike out to-night!"

"Apologize to Cull Cole!" repeated the old foreman, hate throbbing through his words. "For what—shootin' our men? *His* ain't hurt. He was tres-

passin' our range—*cow* range! By Jiminy, I'd see
him in the hot place, before I'd apologize to a——"

"All right, Cim," Dare soothed him. "We'll let it
ride to-night—— Listen," he cried tensely, "ain't
that shots off there—north of El Capitan?"

Together they listened, their faces turned toward
the great mount bulking awful and mysterious against
the sky, placed there by God, as a constant reminder
of the nothingness of man. But they could distinguish only the faint and far-off rumble of the retreating storm.

"Reckon it's thunder," Cim said nervously.
"Reckon we both got shootin' on the brain."

They were silent a moment.

"Somehow," Dare said earnestly, "I've got to go
on with this. I've saddled myself with these folks—
took their money—an' I've got to go on. But there'll
be no more monkeyshines. When this season is over,
I'm runnin' a straight cow ranch. An' from now
on——"

They both heard *this*—hoofs in mad gallop, hoofs
that by the peculiar timing of their beat, even more
than by their fury, betokened something disastrously
amiss! Down along the adobe wall they thundered,
in the gate, and up the drive, bringing the excited
visitors rushing from the house. The light from the
open door fell on a foam-lashed horse and a rider who
grasped the saddle with both hands and weaved. It
was—Cim shouted, springing to the animal's head—
one of Gid Perkins' men!

Dare caught the reeling horseman as he fell.

"It's come!" gasped the rider, gazing wildly around.
"We was goin'—to town. Met Cull Cole's outfit
—a mile outta here. He fired on us. Gave no warn-

in'. Shot us down—like dogs! Boys, rush— help——" He fainted in Dare's arms.

In that instant of wild confusion—filled by Cim's horrible imprecations, by the plunging of horses, as his crew, without waiting for his order, dashed away —Dare saw how this fresh calamity had come to pass. Cull Cole—knowing he was trespassing cattle range, knowing the feeling against him, and believing that he had been attacked by cowmen—had, in the dusk, met Gid Perkins' men and, thinking them to be the same outfit in pursuit, had opened hostilities on them! A natural, a hideous mistake! And Dare's the blame —for not rushing straight to Cull. This blood, too, was on his hands!

Dully, above the black thoughts beating in his brain, rose the shrill screams of Eloise in hysterics, the fluttering cries of the other women trying to quiet her, and the sarcastic voice of Jasper Kade, advising them not to get anguished, that it was probably more of the joke.

And Dare never forgot old Cimarron White, towering over the cynical youth, his eyes blazing, his strained, upflung arms shaking in his passion, nor the awful truth that rang with contempt in his voice as he shouted: "Joke? You pitiful pilgrim, this is no joke! *This is war!*"

CHAPTER X

REMORSE

THOUGH morn had dawned—fresh, summer scented, washed by night showers, almost too glorious under other circumstances to be borne— Cim's cry, "This is war!" rang in Dare's brain still. War! War! War! Check's hoofs beat time to the sinister song as he galloped the Sundown Road. Surely he had dreamed it all! Surely it was some horrible nightmare from which he must awaken! For the country was as still, as peaceful with the great, golden ball of the sun rolling up on the tawny plains, as devoid of the least hint of anything exciting, as on that day when its peace had irked him, riding so jauntily into the range.

Oh, to be as he had been that June day, footloose and free, on his way—anywhere, he had not cared where—with adventure his only goal. To be as he had been but yesterday—could it be but yesterday?— planning excitement for his guests, laughing until he cried as they were getting their first taste of it on the mountain road.

A stranger, seeing Dare Devlyn then, light-hearted, eager, laughing-eyed, and seeing him now, haggard, haunted, would have sworn that years must have elapsed to cause the change. But it was war! It was a foretaste of war that he had had in the long night just ended.

He had not gone to the scene of battle—for he had had a battle at the ranch with Cim. He could not bear to think yet of his fight with the foreman. The old fire eater had gone berserk. He would have gone after the sheepmen, massacred them, had he not been held by force, until his brain cooled, and the voice of reason could make itself heard. And when that time came, the boys had returned with the red grist of war!

All night Dare had handled it, working beside the doctor, until, like Eloise, he was faint at the sight of blood. Many of Gid Perkins' riders had been wounded. The five worst injured were still at Corral de Terra, and the bunk house was a hospital. It was not known whether Cull Cole had suffered any casualties or not; probably not, for he had taken the cowmen by surprise. If so, he had moved his own injured.

And dawn had brought word that Gid Perkins had gone berserk, too; but, yielding to cooler counsel, had gone to town to swear out a warrant against Cull Cole. So, instead of taking the rest he needed, Dare was on his way to Sundown to prevent *that* mistake, to tell the sheriff the whole story, absolve every one else of blame, and take what was coming to him.

Cim had raised the roof about this, too, Dare reflected, had tried to stop him, made fun of him. But this time he wasn't listening to Cim! If he had gone straight to Cull when he first meant to, when Cim first stopped him, this last, worst crisis need not have occurred.

Swinging into Sundown, Dare's fear that he was hours too early to find any one astir was allayed with shocking swiftness. For Sundown was awake and stirring, as he had never seen it. Horses jammed the street, and armed, grim-faced men lined the curb. Knots of plainsmen and townsmen, gathered on every corner, heatedly discussed the attack. All were cowmen—a circumstance ominous in itself.

"Cole was invadin' cow range—movin' that mutton toward the Rio!" cried a huge, swarthy fellow. "That's mighty bold——"

Hoarse, fierce threats, a torrent of wrath drowned his words.

"Men," called a bronzed rancher indignantly, "Hooker trailed his danged woollies past my place afore sunrise to join Cole!"

"Rallyin' round the flag, huh!" jeered a third. "You savvy what that means! They'll concentrate up there, ready to cross the Rio an' crowd us out! But with Corral de Terra back in the saddle, we'll——" He stopped.

The speaker in every tense group also stopped, as though sight of that oddly checked, black-and-white paint pony were a tap to turn off words.

Dare was acutely conscious of this silence that fell at his approach, of the babble that rose behind him. "There goes the fool to blame for it!" his guilty conscience told him they were saying. And shame seared his soul. Eyes seemed to bore him through.

But with his resolution firm upon him, he pulled Check up before the sheriff's office, slid to the curb, and was crossing the sidewalk, when he was instantly hailed from the nearest group.

Turning impatiently, he saw an old ranger approaching. Suddenly it struck him how strangely all these Los Lobos old-timers looked alike—enough alike to be brothers. All were fierce-eyed as old pumas; all had the same cold quality of steel and ice. And Dare had the guilty feeling that he was in for recrimination, or further warnings such as he had had from Kit Kress and Cim. So he was amazed when the old fellow stretched out his hand, saying with hearty deference: "Put 'er there!"

Taking the boy's hand in a grip as hearty as his voice, the old man continued: "I tell you, Devlyn, us cowmen sure admire your way of doin' things. All we needed was a man with gumption to take the lead, a man big enough to fill the Jessimers' boots. An' you sure fill 'em! That move you made was worthy of Lynne Jessimer himself! We're backin' you to a man. Put 'er there ag'in!"

Stunned by this—the worst mistake of all—Dare hurriedly protested: "But I ain't fillin' the Jessimers' boots! I ain't leadin' any one! What I done was just a joke——"

"By the Lord Harry," exclaimed his admirer, as other cowmen swarmed about Dare, "you're all right, Devlyn! You ain't topheavy—though the brains you showed would warrant it! We like the quiet way you went about this—sawed wood an' said nothin'! Got a hold of the ol' ranch an' waded in. Let us razz you like boobs, call you a dude rancher! Ha-ha! Say, if we'd 'a' handled the sheepmen like you did—opened up on 'em the minit they trespassed our range—we wouldn't be facin' this issue! If what you done was a joke, we'd sure like to see what you'd do——"

Roughly, Dare broke away. This, then, was why they stared. They thought he had deliberately started this war against the sheepmen. They had brought up all his old talk of excitement to prove it. He would not stand it! He would not have folks thinking that! He would tell his story to the sheriff—then they'd know!

Quickly, Dare mounted the steps to Sheriff Hardy's office. He had his hand on the knob, when the door burst open, and a highly excited man, whom he recognized as the deputy sheriff, stormed out, bearing a suit case.

"Is the sheriff in?" Dare stopped him with a question.

The fellow turned on him almost truculently, saw who he was, and seemed unduly surprised.

"No!" he exploded. "An' it wouldn't do *you* any good if he was!"

"Well," Dare said wearily, "you'll do—you're deputy."

The man laughed jarringly. "Not now—I ain't! I just threw up my star. Devlyn"—his voice caught in his very earnestness—"I've rode cow range since I was knee high to a centipede. I ain't changin' my spots none to hold my job! I'm a cowman to the core, an' the sheriff——"

"Listen!" Dare broke in with sudden fear. "Has Hardy gone to serve that warrant on Cull Cole?"

Again came that jarring laugh. "Has Hardy gone to arrest Cole? Say, that's rich! Not much! That's why I quit. Gid Perkins tears into town afore sunup, routs Prosecutor Holt out of bed, an' swears out a warrant for Cole—chargin' his outfit with assault with intent to kill. He brings the warrant to Hardy, but the sheriff refuses to serve it, sayin' the cowmen started the fuss. Smack on that, Cull Cole ramps in, wantin' a warrant for Perkins on the same charge, an' Holt refuses to issue it—sayin' the sheepmen did

the shootin'. So the machinery of the law is dead-
locked. Hardy's up at Holt's office now, havin' it
out with him."

"You mean," asked Dare, a hundred fearful con-
jectures spinning in his mind, "that the sheriff an'
prosecuting attorney are passin' the buck? Both
shyin' off from the responsibility?"

"I don't!" was the warm denial. "They're both
good men. They're both doin' their duty as they see
it. But each sees it different. Just electin' a man to
office don't make him a diplomat, a demigod, or a
owl-eyed prophet. The human equation's still there.
Hardy owns a big interest in the Three Star Ranch—
sheep. Holt is silent partner in the Seven Up outfit—beef. There you are—an' a purty kittle of fish,
if you ask me!"

It seemed so to Dare. It seemed that Fate was
bent on carrying on the tragic jest. But it occurred
to him that if he could find the officers together,
he could make them see straight. And, looking
neither to left nor right lest he be halted again, he
hurried the half block to Holt's office.

Sheriff Hardy was still there, for even before
Dare reached the door, he heard them in hot dis-
cussion. So heatedly rose their voices that his repeated knocks were drowned. Too anxious to stand
on ceremony, Dare opened the door and went in.

Belligerently, the two men in whose hands lay
the fate of the Los Lobos range were facing each
other across Holt's desk, their faces red and hot,
their glances seeming to shoot sparks as they clashed.
They were far too engrossed to note Dare, standing
just inside the door, white and unhappy, hat twisted
in his nervous hands.

"You'll serve this warrant," Prosecutor Holt threatened, waving a document under Sheriff Hardy's nose, "or we'll get a man who will!"

"Go to it!" Hardy dared him. "I'm here by the will of the people. Only the people can recall me. I'm here to serve the people, *all the people*—not just one faction! Nor am I here to persecute one faction! You make out a warrant for Gid Perkins, an' see how quick I serve that!"

Holt glared at him, purpling. "I'm not here to issue warrants on misused citizens! I want the man to blame for this outrage."

Quite simply then, quite without dramatic intent, Dare said miserably: "I'm the man."

They started at his voice, angry at his intrusion, at what he had heard, and were startled into listening to what he had come to say.

Dare told how he had arranged the sham battle to entertain the Easterners at Corral de Terra; how the sheep he had hired had failed to appear on time, and how Cull Cole's band had so unfortunately happened along. He told how his men had mistakenly fired on Cole's followers with blanks, and how they, not understanding, had returned the fire with lead; how Cole, then, meeting Gid Perkins' outfit and doubtless believing them to be the attacking cowmen in pursuit, had opened fire on them. No crime, Dare, said, had been committed by either Cole or Perkins; no man was even remotely to blame but himself. And when he was done, he saw, to his despair, that the faces of his listeners were as cold and uncompromising as before.

"Devlyn," Holt said coldly, "you're takin' yourself a heap too serious. We aren't interested in your shenanigans out there. Allow it all—and it's no extenuation for Cole's shooting down cowmen, going peaceably about their own business. Cull Cole's no fool! This trouble was brewing long before you came upon the secne, and he saw his chance to bring things to head. Now—you've had your say. You're interrupting a business meeting. Get out!"

"Yeah," sarcastically Hardy added benediction, "trot along an' sin no more! Every one knows where Corral de Terra stands!"

Holt turned on the speaker wrathfully. "Do you mean to infer that this kid is to blame for last night's trouble?"

"No!" bluntly rejoined the sheriff. "I infer that you wouldn't arrest him if he was—him bein' a cowman! He's no more to blame than Cull Cole, so I ain't arrestin' Cole. I don't intend to fill the jail with sheepmen, board 'em at the people's expense for gosh knows how long, an' leave the real culprits— *cowmen*—rangin' free!"

Abruptly, Holt swung on Dare. "Devlyn, this promises to be personal. Clear out!"

All but thrown out, Dare returned to Check. And, undecided what to do next, he found himself lovingly mobbed by an excited group of cow partisans.

"We're with you, Devlyn!" they roared, fighting to take his hand, clap his back, touch his person or his horse.

"We'll herd the woollies back on their own reservation!"

"No, by gravy," swore a furious voice, "we'll wipe 'em off the Los Lobos range!"

Almost in terror, Dare bolted from them and spurred madly out of town.

"He's deep," one said, after Dare had gone, "still an' deep."

"Waal," said another, "that's the kind it takes!"

"The Jessimer kind!" struck in a third. "Say, who is this boy? Where'd he come from? Don't it strike you queer that he happened along on Corral de Terra just at this time?"

"By George, there's something in that!" clamored another. "Boys, he looks enough like Lynne Jessimer to be his son! He *might* be Lynne's son! What do we know about Lynne, after he——"

"A Jessimer!" cheered some one wildly. "Boys, the Los Lobos is saved for beef!"

So they built up a personality for Dare—one reflected by the martial spirit of the old ranch and its old owners. Fancy was stated for fact. The wildest speculation was taken for truth. And it was generally understood that Dare, some kin of the Jessimers, had taken over Corral de Terra with the sole purpose of leading the Los Lobos in this war whose red-hot breath, like wildfire, was already sweeping the plains.

But Dare's only thought now was to put out the fire he had kindled. He decided to take the truth to Gid Perkins and Cull Cole. He arrived at this decision just as he came within sight of Corral de Terra, and reining in—to realize with shame how wildly he had been riding, for Check was a lather of sweat—he saw Kit Kress jogging slowly toward him in a buckboard. His shame deepened at the thought of how lightly he had treated the agent's warning yesterday, and all that had come of it. But there was no reproach in Kit's face; in fact, he avoided all mention of the trouble.

"I've been out to the ranch," he said, his eyes fixed on the whipsocket. "Took out Jim Grant an' Madge."

Dare stared at him in dismay. Jim Grant—the man who did not want excitement! In all that had happened since Kit announced their coming yesterday, these new guests had slipped his mind. They were old friends of Kit's, too!

"Kit," he said contritely, "I plumb forgot!"

Kress understood that. He said, "I've talked to Cim. You'll find him docile now, son." Then, after a long scrutiny of the boy's worn face, he added: "Don't take this too much to heart. Remember, you're not to blame for this here hiatus. You just brought things to a head."

"They think I done it a-purpose!" Dare's eyes smarted at this unexpected sympathy. "They think I'm leadin' 'em in a war against the sheepmen!"

Kit nodded slowly. "Of course. They've prayed for a leader. They think one's been raised. I was afraid of this when you bought Corral de Terra. It's natural for Los Lobos cowmen to look to the old ranch for lead. But"—and he was very earnest—"don't let them stampede you into it, son."

Dare vowed he would not, and as Kit plucked the reins as if to drive on, disclosed his intention to seek out Perkins and Cole. But, to his astonishment, Kit vetoed that plan as vehemently as Cim had done.

"They wouldn't believe you, son! Gid was in my office this mornin', ringin' your praises. I told him the simple facts of the case. But he laughed at how you'd pulled the wool over my eyes, too! Son, men believe what they *want* to believe. Perkins wants to believe in the resurrection of the old spirit of Corral

de Terra. Cull Cole don't want to believe he's made
a fool of himself. He wouldn't believe your attack
wasn't hostile. Take my advice: Lay low, an' say
nothin'. Tend to your own affairs. I'd say you had
your hands full—with a hotel an' a hospital both out
there! An' pray to heaven this cloud blows over."

And Dare, who had rejected Kit's advice once—
and had had such bitter cause to rue it—promised
to take it now.

They parted. Dare galloped on, along the high
ranch wall, through the gate, and came upon a tableau
that seared itself forever on his brain.

A man stood in the flowery court, where birds
spilled their liquid, golden notes, and flowers splashed
their color. A gray man he was, gray haired, gray
bearded, dressed in quiet gray, and his face, lifted to
El Capitan, on which the morning sun flowed now
like molten gold, was gray with suffering. It was
suffering that beat him down, for, even as Dare's eyes
took in the scene, the gray man crumpled to his knees,
threw up his hands before his face, and began praying monotonously, solemnly:

"God help me! God help me! God give me
strength!"

A girl, with pale-gold hair and deep-blue eyes,
and a face that was Dare's conception of an angel's,
bent over him, crying: "Oh, father, don't! I told
you—you shouldn't have come."

"Madge, I *had* to come! I didn't think I'd feel
—like this! But it all—don't worry, girl. It's—all
right. Just give me—time!"

Warned by some subtle sense that strange eyes
were on them, Madge Grant looked about and saw
Dare Devlyn.

"The trip has been too much for him," she said quietly. "Please help me get him to his room."

And Dare felt that he would have died for the privilege and pleasure of helping Madge Grant! From their first meeting, he trod roseate clouds instead of earth. Madge Grant was all and more, that he had expected Eloise to be. Exquisite, exotic, she charmed, dazzled him by the very things that placed her so far beyond him. His old interest in his venture flamed anew. His flowering love for Allie Boone was choked out by the star dust of the new.

If, at that moment, war was crowded to the far horizon of Dare's mind, surely there was excuse! He was young, full of fire, riding the top wave of life. After all, he couldn't live *always* with remorse.

CHAPTER XI

"A RANGE MAN!"

WHEN Jim Grant appeared at lunch he had fully recovered from the bad effects of his trip. Dare could hardly believe him to be the same man he had seen in the court. Despite his gray hair and beard, there was nothing infirm in his appearance. On the contrary, he impressed the boy by his singular vigor and force. His keen, deep-set, black eyes— "X-raying eyes," a business rival once called them— seemed to see right through the person they rested on. His manner was quiet and unobtrusive. But the little he said was spoken in a way that compelled attention and respect, and from the moment he sat down at the table, he dominated it strangely as though he, and not Dare Devlyn, were host.

To Dare, Grant's coming was a godsend. For his guests, cruelly shocked by the tragedy of last night, were on the point of immediate departure. In fact, the Hiltons had been so satiated with thrills coming out to the ranch that they had not left their rooms since. But Jim Grant's presence seemed to link the rest with the conventional existence they had left, and to assure them that all was still right with the world. For, to Dare's surprise, they all knew Grant by reputation.

"Why, he's one of the biggest promoters in America!" Eloise confided in an excited whisper. "He handled Coral Strand—you know, that exclusive millionaire resort. I'm simply thr-rilled to be under the same roof with him!"

Ezra Biggers was no less impressed, and he pridefully unearthed a dozen mutual acquaintances during the meal. Mrs. Mills discovered that a Schenectady club friend was the mother of one of Madge Grant's schoolmates, and straightway adopted a maternal attitude toward the girl that was touching. This was maddening to the sensible mother, who foresaw great things to come of this summer contact between Jim Grant's girl and her own daughter, Hortense. Only their personal interest in the newcomers prevented their noting the helpless condition of Dare.

In spite of the mental and physical strain that youth labored under, he could not tear his gaze from Madge Grant, and his heart was in his eyes as he stared at her, sitting across the table from him, eating so daintily, talking so easily, looking so lovely! Already, she was a beautiful fever in his blood, taking away his appetite, distorting his vision, making him irrational in his acts, and apt as not on the least provocation to rave deliriously of blue eyes and golden hair. And there was no cure for Dare! He knew it. She was miles above him—so high that he could never hope to climb to her. But he could look up at her in humble worship, and he did.

When lunch was over, Dare was about to hunt out a quiet spot and dream of Madge, when he met the Hiltons in the hall, bag and baggage—not icicles now, but hot all over—demanding immediate conveyance to Sundown so that they could catch to-day's train, and be transported far from that madhouse! Dare was only too glad to comply. But he resented the thousand and one other duties that claimed his mind. Duties which he considered beneath a man's attention, but which he might have foreseen, when he stepped out of his line to be a landlord—a job compared to which, he now saw, punching cows was a cinch.

He had to rustle Eloise a lamp and a curling iron —in lieu of a beauty parlor—for her hair was "a sight." Mrs. Mills waylaid him with a bundle to be sent to the French laundry! He told her there was only one laundry in the Los Lobos, and it was Chinese. She would have to patronize it, or rub her own. Josefa threw a tantrum in the kitchen—calling upon all her saints to witness that she had but one pair of hands, and how could one pair of hands hope to feed so many? Dare yanked in a highly mutinous waddy to flunky for her, valiantly wrestled with Hortense's window, since she could not sleep a wink without fresh air, and by the time he had pacified Ezra Biggers with a promise of grapefruit for breakfast on the morrow—provided such high-toned fodder could be had in Sundown—he was ready to take a good, long jump at himself.

Instead, he visited his patients—a misnomer, if ever there was one! The Perkins riders were doing as well as possible, and their boss was sending rigs that afternoon to take them home. Las Vegas was going to pull through. A tight squeeze, but he'd make it, the doctor said, and that blessed news lifted a mountainous weight off Dare. Sam, outraged at being confined to bed with a flesh wound, was cross as a bear with a sore head. He wouldn't have any more folks popping in on him, coddling and pitying him, so help him Israel!

Mace, up and about, with his arm bandaged, was showing Jim Grant over the place. And old Cim— considerably toned down by whatever Kit Kress had said to him—was trailing the pair. In fact, Corral de Terra's foreman seemed as fascinated by Jim Grant as its owner had been by Grant's daughter. He couldn't seem to take his eyes from him—even when, now and then, he removed his sombrero to scratch his head, a sure sign of tall thinking in Cim.

And Dare, free for the moment, was crossing the court with the intention of joining them, when he suddenly thought of Allie, and remembered with a sharp twinge of conscience that he had not had time to be civil to her. And she was such a proud little thing! Swap had pitched his tent down by the river again. Dare decided that he had better go down and insist on their moving up to the house as he had first planned. Allie had dreamed of being the little lady of this big house, and he must not let her be overlooked in the shuffle. She could be a big help to him, take a lot off his mind.

Accordingly, he was going around the house when Cim nabbed him.

"Son," whispered the old fellow mysteriously, "if that State of Mainer's a dude, I'm a sure-enough Hopi medicine man!"

"Why, what else could he be?" Dare grinned.

Firmly Cim said: "That hombre's a range man!"

"You're loco!" The boy laughed outright. "Jim Grant's a big promoter. Ezra knows folks he knows. So does Mrs. Mills."

"So do I!" Cim said stubbornly. "Kit knows him. Kit an' him is almighty thick. I seen that when they drove in. Where could Kit Kress meet a big promoter?"

Dare was curious about that himself. Still, as he reminded Cim, Kress was in a position, as land agent, to meet all kinds of folks.

"Uh-huh!" Cim conceded. "But that don't account for Grant's gait none. Lookit it, son," he urged, as the man in question walked slowly by with Mace. "You notice he don't slink like that Buff'lar Jasper, nor waddle, like Biggers. He sorta—*teeters!* Son, that hombre learned to walk on high heels!"

"Nonsense, Cim."

"Besides," Cim insisted, "he's got range savvy. Oh, he don't know nothin' about anything, but when Mace explains it, he sees the point like a range man sees it."

"He's smart, Cim," the boy said idly.

"Yeah"—slowly Cim conceded that also—"he's smart. He—he puts me in mind of somebody—I'm most crazy thinkin' who!" As though drawn by an invisible leash, he moved after Jim Grant.

But Dare did not go on to Swap's. While talking to Cim, he had seen Allie down by the river gate with Jasper Kade. They were there yet. And, standing under the sycamores, watching them, Dare frowned as he remembered that Jasper had been with Allie last night—and every time he had seen her since. He did not like it—the way that smooth shorthorn was hanging around Allie. The dude sure had took a swift interest in life. He acted as tickled as a small boy with a new red wagon. And she was just a romantic, little kid.

He did not see their parting—maneuvered by Allie when she saw Dare, in the breathless hope that he would join her. He did not see her shyly lingering there, clinging to that hope. He did not see her start and brighten—a little flame, in her red-calico dress, against the green of distant cottonwoods— as he stepped her way, nor the cloud that came over her as she saw her mistake.

For Dare had seen only the miracle of Madge Grant, seated on the arbored bench under the river wall, gayly beckoning to him. And it was to *her* he was going, feeling so gawky, under the scrutiny of her friendly, blue eyes. He was painfully aware of the *swish, swish* of his wide-winged chaps, the creak of his calfskin boots, the glitter of his silver-ware, his silk shirt and all—things he had been so proud of when he had made his splurge. As silly, he thought now, as Allie's idea of a red-velvet dress for garden wear. It was odd that he could see how silly that was now; odd, too, that he could not see Allie being irresistibly drawn to that same bench.

"Sit down." Smilingly Madge patted it in invitation. "And tell me—did you toil for them or did you spin?"

Dare's fingers tightened about his sombrero's brim, and hot color swept his face. He did not know what she meant, but he knew she was making fun of him.

"Because," she said, smiling at his confusion, "Solomon in all his glory was not arrayed——"

"Oh, *these!*" Dare made a violent gesture, as though to divest himself of the glorious raiment forthwith.

"Please, don't!" she laughed. "The male *should* be the gorgeous sex. But the only place I've seen the male of the human species use his prerogative is in the West. You can't imagine how refreshing it is. I like it."

Gee, Dare was glad she liked it! He would break in that pink shirt to-morrow. And, with a sincerity that must have been as refreshing to Madge as its tense utterance was surprising, he burst out :

"I sure like your dress!"

Manlike, he did not notice a thing about it, except that it was white, with dashes of gold to match her hair and the wild sunflowers nodding all about. But none of its simple elegance was wasted on Allie's eyes—straining in love and jealousy from out the vines, nor did her ears fail to catch the singing lilt in Dare's voice as he asked:

"You ain't been West before?"

No, this was her first trip, Madge told him in the natural, unaffected way that was no small part of her charm. But her father had been West before— when he was young.

That was how he had met Kit, then, thought Dare.

"We were all packed to spend a vacation at our Adirondack camp, when father got Kit Kress' letter telling about Corral de Terra, and he was wild to come."

It was strange that such a life should appeal to a man who did not want excitement, and strange that the thought did not occur to Dare. But he was thinking how strange it was that he—a common puncher—should know a girl like Madge!

Quite without knowing how it came about, he told her how he had fallen heir to twelve thousand dollars when he was just a forty-a-month waddy down on the Pecos, and had forthwith set out to meet adventure halfway. He told how he had happened on the lonely ruins of the old ranch, met Allie——

Unconsciously, he broke off, staring so absorbedly at her crowning glory—the very phrase for it!—that when she laughingly demanded his thoughts, she got the truth, the whole truth, and nothing but the truth:

"Your head—it looks like a sunflower!"

Swiftly she dropped her eyes, reaching for one of the golden blobs, nodding near. But he had seen the laughter in them.

"I mean," he stammered wretchedly, "it's yellow—like them. They're clown flowers to some folks, but I—I like them—next to lupines."

She felt sorry for him. "Lots of people like them," she helped him out. "You know what one great poet said about them:

"'As the sunflower turns to her god when he sets
The same look which she turned when he rose.'"

"Meanin'," Dare said quickly, "that they turn their heads to watch the sun? But they don't. It's pretty, but it ain't true."

She smiled again at how literal he was, and he, thinking she smiled at his break, made it worse by blurting: "But your hair—it's both—pretty an' real and——"

In human mercy, she changed the subject. "Who is Allie?" she asked.

Forgetting himself in this interesting theme—unaware that every word was a knife thrust through the sensitive heart of Allie Boone—Dare told the lovely patrician beside him just who Allie was. A poor, little girl kid, who had been born in a wagon, brought up in a wagon, and was heartbroken because folks called her a wagon tramp. He told Madge how he had first met Allie, dressed up in an old Navajo blanket and lupine wreath, playing lady in the wrecked old house, how she wanted to be a lady, and studied in movies and "The Fatal Wedding"——

"A movie, too?" Madge was intrigued.

"No—a book!" Dare's dark face glowed with the light of a great idea. "But if she could just be around the real thing—a girl like you," he said earnestly, "why, she'd pick it up in no time! She's a born mimic, an' she does so much with the little she has to do with—— Why, she ain't even got a name, like other girls! She's called for a town—Albuquerque! Poor kid. Reckon I bought Corral de Terra as much to give Allie a chance as anything."

Madge gave him the strangest look. Already she suspected what Dare must learn in the agony of the night swiftly hurtling toward them—a night that might have been a black page plucked from the past's sad history—the night when, after years of silence, the Los Lobos range would ring again to the old battle cry of the Jessimers!

"How old is Allie?" she asked.

"Seventeen." If only she *would* take an interest in Allie, Dare thought. "But you'd never think it. She's just a barelegged little kid. Pretty as a picture, if she had a chance. But she has to live in a dirty camp, wear ol' overalls, an' calico rags——"

There was a sound in the vine behind them—the cry of a wild thing wounded mortally, that yet must hush its agony lest it be discovered and tortured further before death comes! And Allie dragged herself, like a wounded, wild thing, down to the sanctuary of the river camp.

CHAPTER XII

"DRUG-STORE BLONDE!"

THE old covered wagon, the *Santa Maria,* was all the home Allie had ever known. Motherless from infancy, its rocking on strange roads had cradled her. From sun and storm, its grimy, canvas wall had sheltered her. But no storm that had ever racked it was half so devastating to the girl it sheltered as this storm of shame and tortured love that she now went through within its kindly wings.

Mercifully, few possess such a capacity for suffering as Allie—undisciplined, primitive, passionate child of nature that she was. Only those who harbor the memory of some little vagrant in their own poor pasts can possibly appreciate the agonies she had endured in her short lifetime from slights and ridicule, both fancied and real. Only these may understand how Dare's pity, his avowal that he had done what he had done because he was sorry for her, scorched her soul with searing waves of shame. Every word he had told Madge was true. But truth hurts when it holds shame; it is killing when it cannot be helped.

And Allie could not help it. She could not remember the day when she had not known that there was something wrong with their way of living, when she had not begged her father to change it and live like other folks. But Swap could not see anything wrong with it. He liked it! *He* pitied folks who lived in houses! And he did not mind—did not *see* —the snickers and stares that greeted the old wagon wherever it went. He did not see how Allie shrank from them, as her beauty-loving nature shrank from the misfit, unlovely garments that were her portion.

"Unto every one that hath, shall be given—but from him that hath not, shall be taken away even that which he hath." So it has been written; so, in Allie's case, the unjust rule worked out. In Allie's eyes, Madge Grant had everything, and, because she had everything, she was given Dare's love also.

Never had Allie felt so desolate, so degraded, stripped of the last vestige of self-respect. She was herself vain, silly, and ridiculous in the sight of Dare, always to be compared to Madge—the "real thing"—and she wanted to run away—hide!

For the first time in her life, she wanted to be on the road—leaving Corral de Terra. Oh, why didn't Swap come and hitch up, and go! She wanted to go where Dare could not ever see her, ever pity her again. And in the same sobbing breath, Allie knew that she would not go now if she could. She would not run away! Oh, if she could only dress up— *beautiful*—show him that she was pretty, too—even if her head didn't look like a sunflower!

"Oh, I hate her!" she moaned, as a spasm of sobs seemed tearing the heart right out of her. "I hate him, too!"

But she took that back. She didn't hate Dare— she loved him! She'd kissed him! A shameful thought that burned like a coal of fire. And he'd just been sorry for her! Wildly she cried, as on that day she had kissed him, when Dare had begged her to stay:

"Oh, I wisht I was dead! I wisht I was dead!"

And that distracted wish—uttered in a queer, strangled voice that was not Allie's, struck dismay on Swap's ear, as he came up from the creek with fishing pole and catch. Dropping both, he bounded up the bank, clambered into the *Santa Maria,* to find Allie face down on her little bed, weakly beating her clenched fists on the pillow, gasping for breath.

"Allie, what is it?" he pleaded, frightened out of his wits.

Seeing that she could not answer, he lifted her in his arms and carried her out of the hot wagon to the cool shade of the river trees. There, sitting in the grass, he held her quivering form tight to his old hickory shirt, a light of love on his sun-browned, whiskery face that was redemption for every crooked deal he had ever made. Brushing the damp curls from her soft, hot cheeks as tenderly as though she were his motherless baby still, he pleaded over and over frantically:

"Baby—tell pop!"

"Oh, my dress!" she gasped. "This—ol' calico rag!"

Swap almost dropped her in his relief.

"Why, what's wrong with it?" He was honestly bewildered. "It's a right purty dress. An' it ain't old, Allie—not that one. No hand-me-down about it a-tall. No, siree! I *bought* that, Allie—good, turkey-red caliker, right off the bolt! A nice, sensible dress, strikes me. Don't show the dirt——"

She could have screamed at that. "Oh, pop," she wept, her eyes so big they scared Swap, "can't you

see? I look like a scarecrow. I ain't got a *real*
dress, pop! And *she* could change hers seventeen
times a day. She——"

"Who's she?" Swap Boone was seeing the light.

"Madge Grant—the new girl!" Allie sobbed. "I
ain't got no clothes, pop, an' she's got *trunks* full!
Oh, pop"—her wild longing would have touched a
harder heart than Swap's—"if I had just *one* decent
outfit! If I could look like other girls—like *her*—
once!"

Then her grief gave way to terror at certain de-
cisive movements on the part of Swap. He set her
down in the grass, straightened up, and hitching his
galluses—his way of girding his loins for battle—
stepped briskly toward the wagon.

"Pop!" she screamed. "Don't do that! I'll die
of shame. Don't you dare trade her out of a dress!
I wouldn't wear it, pop! I'll run away! I'll——"

"But, honey"—Swap turned, bewildered—"it's
legitimate! If she's got more glad rags than she kin
wear, she'll mebbe be glad to swap one fer the
cuckoo——"

"Pop!" That fierce ejaculation stayed him,
brought him slowly back. And terrified lest in mis-
taken kindness he put this last, crushing humiliation
on her, Allie tried to make him understand.

"Clothes ain't all!" she cried tragically. "It's who
she is, an' what I am—dirt under her feet!"

A flame flashed in the trader's eye. His very
whiskers bristled. "Did she call you that?"

"No! No!" Allie protested, reaching up a restrain-
ing hand. "But she's Jim Grant's girl. *Everybody*
knows Jim Grant!"

A certain complacence softened Swap's face and,

sitting down beside her again, he said with a certain pride: "Allie, if there's any man in these here United States of America what's got a wider acquaintance than your own pop, I——"

"That's it!" she said desperately. "Can't you see, pop? It's how we're known! Everybody—from Kansas Bluff to Fresno—knows what *we* are! But the Grants—they're somebody! Madge's family——"

"Allie," Swap said severely, "don't forget you're a Boone!"

She could not forget it—ever, she knew.

"The Boones can hold up their heads with the best of 'em," continued Swap seriously. "We're a mighty proud breed. We call no man master. We ain't beholden to any man! An' when it comes to family —waal, ours runs back to Adam, an' it ain't on a decline, like some of 'em! Your grandpop, Hez Boone, was some persimmons around Hickory Springs, Arkansas. He owned two hundred acres of vallyable soil, an' raised two thousand pounds of seed cotton to the acre. On top of that, he was a water witch!"

Allie was torn between laughter and tears. It was no use—her father just could not understand.

"If this Grant gal rings in a family tree on you," Swap instructed his offspring, "head yours with grandpop. If *he* don't squelch her—why, there's Daniel!"

"In the lion's den!" Allie giggled, wholly hysterical.

"Daniel Boone!" Swap frowned at her levity. "I reckon even the Grants has heard tell of Daniel."

"But he ain't no kin to us," Allie scoffed, wide-eyed.

"Mebbe not," admitted the old trader. "But," shrewdly, "nobody kin prove he ain't! Personally, I allus thought I had p'ints in common with Daniel—favored him some, too, in looks. So, buck up, baby. You don't have to take a back seat for the Queen of Sheba! Nor back talk, neither!" He could not get it out of his head that she had been insulted. "If we choose to tote our merchandise from place to place, catchin' business where it's briskest, why, that's good business judgment. I'm a business man. An' when it comes to that," he wound up proudly, "I reckon I kin dress my gal just as fine as Jim Grant's!"

Cautiously he looked all about him, between trees, and up the trail to Corral de Terra. Then, dropping his voice cautiously, he said:

"Allie, we ain't poor folks. This here Jim Grant ain't such a much! Your own pop's made money, too, this season. *Big* money, Allie—I've got fifty-seven bucks in my pocket right now!"

Her incredulous gasp was all he expected, and with boyish delight in her surprise, he fished out out his greasy old wallet and counted the bills and chicken feed into her lap. Then, putting it all back, he placed the wallet and its astounding contents in her rough little hands.

"You take it, honey," he said eagerly. "Git you a new outfit. Git the best money kin buy—if it takes it all. Put out 'er eye!"

Tears of a happier kind filled Allie's eyes. She suspected that Madge's dress alone cost fifty dollars —she would have been as astonished as Swap to have known how very much more it cost. But she was too touched by this proof of his love for her to tell him. He had offered her his last cent. He was a

good man—as good as Jim Grant. She did not need
to be ashamed of him—or of herself. She would not
try to be something she was not. She would hold
her head up with the rest of the Boones!

"Thanks, pop," she said quietly, as she handed it
back. "I don't need a new dress. This one is fine
—for a camp. It don't—show the dirt."

Swap's eyes opened to their widest, and his jaw
dropped. "Waal," he ejaculated fervently, "if wimmin don't beat the Dutch!"

Later, still shaking his head in vain ponderings over
the vagaries of women, Swap went down to the
creek.

"Hey, Allie," he called back, "I gotta fine mess of
trout. You scale 'em, while I stake out the hosses."
He added jocosely: "Betcha Jim Grant's gal can't
scale a fish!"

Allie's wistful "No, pop," was a long time coming.
And Swap, waiting strangely intent for it, saw her
stoop and thrust something into the camp fire.

"Whatcha burnin', Allie?"

"Nothin'," she said drearily. "Nothin'—but trash.
Just—'The Fatal Wedding.' "

But it was more. It was her dreams—her one
escape from the sordid, lonely grind of her existence
—that Allie destroyed. And the act symbolized a
woman's patient acceptance of her lot. Some faint
understanding of this must have been granted Swap,
for though the book was negotiable—worth two bits
in trade—he did not say a word.

Down on her knees, scaling fish—a task she had
once loathed, but now found a new pride in per-
forming—Allie looked up and saw Dare.

She could not know how lovely she was, with her dark beauty set off by the red dress, in such colorful contrast to the green of grass and trees, and the night of her hair, storm-tossed about the sad, pale little moon of her face. She could not know that this view of her—bringing up in his memory that night at Swap's camp fire—brought back Dare's old feeling for her, a feeling strengthened in the months she had been away by memory of her wild kiss and embrace. She could not know that he was thrilling at that memory now, though he had just come from Madge. She only knew that Dare—who had seemed to her a knight in shining armor come out of the books she had forsaken to rescue her from this squalid clutter that surrounded her wherever the old wagon stopped—was sorry for her, pitied her, as he had told Madge.

"I've come, Allie"—the boy's tired face lighted with joy at what was in store for her—"to take you out of this! You an' Swap must move right up to the house. You're to be my li'le housekeeper, remember? I sure need you to ride herd on the women-folks," he said anxiously.

She dried her hands on the clean flour sack that did duty for a towel, and rose, seeming older, taller, in the new dignity that had come to her with the storm.

"Thanks, Dare," she said quietly, "but I ain't goin'. I'd be out of place up there."

"Out of place—*you!*" Loudly, he hooted that, and so sincerely that she had to remember hard that it was pity. "Holy smoke, Allie, no woman ever fitted into that ol' house *but* you! Why, I keep seein' you

like I first seen you—paradin' that ol' hall, givin' orders———"

"Makin' a tomfool of myself," she said bitterly,
her fingers taking tucks in her skimpy dress. "Makin' believe I was a lady. Why, I wasn't even a good
imitation, Dare—but cheap, like my clothes, these
beads!"

"But you could learn, Allie!" The boy's enthusiasm blinded him to the danger signals unfurling in
Allie's cheeks. "Madge Grant wants to help you!
I told her all about you. She said she'd be *glad*
to help! An' you can learn more about bein' a lady
from Madge than from any ol' book."

Madge! Madge! Madge! A storm of jealous
fury flung all Allie's recently acquired poise to the
four winds.

"So I've got to learn, have I?" she raged, white
with pain and anger. "So I ain't good enough to
herd with your high-toned folks, till I learn how to
act! I've got to *learn* to be a lady———"

"Good grief!" Dare exclaimed helplessly. "That's
the way *you* put it! I don't know no more about
ladies 'n a pig does about Sunday—an' care less! I
wouldn't even have noticed how you acted, or what
you had on, if you hadn't called my attention to it!
I'm just tryin' to help you be what you wanted
to be!"

"Go on!" she urged, with a woman's knack of
putting a man in the wrong. "Go on—blame it on
me! *I* don't want to be something I ain't. I'm a
Boone! The Boones can hold up their heads with the
best of 'em!" She demonstrated it by a proud little
lift of her chin. "I don't have to take a back seat
for the Queen of Sheba. An' get this, Mister Dev-

lyn, I ain't takin' no lessons from that—drug-store blonde!''

"Allie!"

It was a wicked fib, but Allie did not care. She was a pirate where her heart was concerned. "Oh, I could have hair like her, if I wanted it!" she cried, and her black eyes blazed disdain. "All I'd have to do is douse peroxide on it! I know! I read it in a beauty hint!"

Even in his horror at this profanation of the heavenly glory of Madge's hair, Dare was horrified to think of Allie bleaching her dusky curls. But Madge's —just thinking of Madge's hair brought up the fever in his blood.

"But your eyes," he raved dreamily, "wouldn't be blue—like hers!"

"I could stand it!" she flashed, knives turning in her heart. "Anyhow, yours ain't brown—like Jasper's!" Fiercely she rejoiced in the rise that got out of him.

"Thank Heaven, they ain't! That hombre's got eyes like a hawk!"

"I like them!" she fibbed, exulting in his fury. "Jasper likes mine, too. He don't want to learn me! He says I'm a wild flower—wastin' my sweetness on the desert air! He says I'm more of a lady than that new girl. Jasper says I'd grace his Gascony château —just as I am!"

"The skunk!" Dare did not know what a "Gascony château" was, but it sounded awful! "Allie, I won't have that smooth-tongued yahoo makin' up to you!"

"Oh, you won't? She laughed in a way that made him ache to shake her—shake this new nonsense out of her. Instead, he caught her slim shoulders and drew her to him.

"Allie," he warned, his earnest gaze bent straight on her, thrilling her, "Jasper Kade ain't like Mace or Las Vegas—the kind of boys you know. He ain't a gentleman like Biggers or Grant. He's no good, Allie!"

"Because he likes me?" she asked coldly.

"Because he lies to you!" Dare cried hotly. "Because he's tryin' to turn your head! Allie, you're the sweetest, best, li'le kid in any man's range, but when he says you're more of a lady than Madge——"

She was like a wild cat then, with her eyes blazing, her red lips drawn back from tiny teeth, her little fists beating his breast, as she fought from him.

It was surprising that the little girl, whom he had thought so frail and weak, could call up such a reserve of fire and strength. It seemed as if every fiber of her being was roused into life by her fury.

"Oh, I hate you!" She whirled in her flight to the tent to scream. "I hate you! Don't you ever speak to me again!"

Completely routed by this display of feminine inconsistency and unreasonableness, Dare left. The victory was Allie's. Never again would he think of her as a child. Never again, even in his maddest infatuation for Madge Grant, could he quite put Allie from his mind. He was certain that she loved Jasper Kade. This only could account for the change in her, and it worried him as nothing had worried him yet.

Why?—he asked himself. Why should he feel responsible for Allie? Wasn't that Swap's lookout? Always Dare's conscience told him that he *was* responsible, just as he was responsible for the wounded men up there, and for this crisis hanging over the Los Lobos range. If he hadn't been a fool, and made a show place of Corral de Terra, this wouldn't have occurred. Allie might have traveled to the end of the road and never met a man like Jasper Kade!

CHAPTER XIII

HIRED GUNS

LATER that same afternoon, Dare, going to the barn, saw two riders striking off across the sunburned slopes back of Corral de Terra. One was Allie, the other, Jasper. Dare's face was clouded with anxiety, when, passing the corral, he beheld a scene that temporarily crowded the riders from his mind.

His men had cut out a bunch of horses and left them standing, saddled, just outside the fence. Among them was a mustang, half wild and wholly vicious, tied hard and fast to the corral gate. And out here, alone, walking among the horses, sizing them up in a critical way, was Jim Grant.

As Dare approached unheard, the man from Maine stopped before the mustang and reached out to stroke his neck. Snorting wildly, the animal jerked back from the contact, pulling against the rope, his ears flattened, his red, rolling eyes watching the man with hate. But without the least sign of timidity, Grant stepped closer and was about to lay his hand on the corded, quivering neck, when the animal reared and struck viciously with both fore hoofs. Coolly, sidestepping the deadly blow, Grant grasped the hackamore as the horse landed, and, holding him down with an iron hand, rubbed his neck, scratched his ears, talked to him quietly, soothingly.

Just like a range man! was the thought that broke like a lightning flash over Dare's mind. But he ridiculed the idea in himself, as he had in Cim. He was getting loco, like the old foreman. All that had happened in the last twenty-four hours, all that might happen, all that Los Lobos folks expected of him, if it did, had raised hob with Dare's nerves. This, and his quarrel with Allie.

Walking back to the house with Grant—forgetting him utterly in his anxious far view of two riders reined close, blending into the blue haze below El Capitan—pain drew Dare's mind to his companion. The pain of Grant's fingers biting into his arm! Looking at Grant, Dare saw that his lean, still face was gray beneath its beard—as it had been when he had ridden upon him in the court—and there was a look in Grant's eyes that reminded him suddenly of Kit Kress, Cim, all the Los Lobos old-timers!

Startled by this thought, Dare followed Grant's gaze to Eloise and Mace. The plump school-teacher was settling her pink ruffles on the edge of the gallery, while Mace, sombrero a-tilt on the back of his head, was aiming the kodak at her a few feet away.

"Are you sure this is the place?" Eloise was chattering. "I want to be able to tell poppa it was snapped right on the spot where Joe Jessimer was killed—— *O-o-oh!* Mace, come here! Isn't this a bloodstain in the wood?"

Deeper the fingers bit into Dare's arm, and Grant's weight sagged on it.

"Looks more like ol' paint," said the prosaic puncher, bending over.

"But it *might* be blood," Eloise hoped. "Be sure it shows in the picture, Mace!"

Weakly, Grant sank down on the bench hard by, unconscious of his clutch that drew Dare down also.

"The morbid fools!" His harsh utterance chilled the boy. "The shallow, heartless, morbid fools!"

Guiltily certain that he was included, Dare said earnestly, "It ain't heartless. It's natural, Grant. It's the nearest thing to excitement some folks have. That's what gave me the idea. That's why I went into this business."

An involuntary shudder ran through him as Grant cried: "It's a ghoulish business! A ghoulish business!" repeated the man, with a passion that awed Dare. "This looting of old graves! A degrading business—pandering to the morbid lusts of a moronic humanity! It's the curse of the age! A man commits an atrocious crime. Immediately he earns more, merely to let people gape at him for a day, than he could have earned by the honorable efforts of a lifetime. Everything he touched, no matter how inconsequential, has morbid interest and value. Is it just? Is it *human?* When I hear of people fighting to see an execution, mobbing a courtroom in a salacious trial, sending flowers to a murderer—Devlyn, why doesn't the Lord repent again of having corrupted the earth with man, and send another flood?"

Through Dare's deep shame and awe ran profound wonder as to why Jim Grant was here—why, if he was not interested in the Jessimers?

"A dangerous business," Grant intoned solemnly, "exploiting a bad reputation—glorifying a bad name!"

But that didn't apply to him, to Corral de Terra, Dare protested. The Jessimers weren't bad! They ought to be remembered—like soldiers! That's what they'd been—soldiers of the range. They had fought for a cause they believed right. In the end they had fought for their lives. And Lynne Jessimer——

"He fought to avenge his brothers. He was a hero, Grant, if ever there was one!"

Grant's eyes closed. "So," he said queerly, "you've made a tin god out of Lynne?"

"He was a man!" warmly persisted Dare. "He was——"

"A dangerous signpost for a lad like you to follow!" even more warmly finished the man from Maine.

A strained silence fell between them. Idly, Dare watched Eloise's pink skirt and Mace's chaps fade into the distance as they moved on to make more pictures. He had the surprised conviction that Mace liked it—being corraled by Eloise! Faintly, voices came to him from behind the gallery vines, where the tourists were assembled, and his pulses leaped to distinguish the low, musical voice of Madge.

"Well," Grant broke in, rising, composed again, "how do you suppose your hero—Lynne—would feel about this? What do you suppose he'd think of strangers holding high carnival where his brothers died, photographing the actual spot, digging bullets out of the walls for souvenirs?"

And suddenly Dare saw his venture in a new light, ghastly light, and self-loathing filled him. "Why," he said bitterly, "he'd think I was a buzzard—feedin' on the dead past of the Jessimers! That's what I am. But—I didn't think!"

"No," Grant's tone was weary, "you didn't think. Neither did I when I was your age. If I had done more thinking at twenty-two, I wouldn't have so much to think of at sixty!" The weight of his thoughts seemed to bow him as they walked on to the house.

And it seemed strangely imperative to Dare to put himself straight with Grant. "I didn't go into this for money," he said eagerly, his eyes imploring belief, "but for excitement, Grant. I got more than I bargained for. I'm 'most loco thinkin' what may come of it yet. I'd quit if I could, but I've got a bear by the tail an' I can't let go!"

Touched by that, by the sick misery in the boy's face, Grant said kindly: "Boy, you're played out. Take a nap, an' forget this."

Forget it—if he only could! "I can't lie down on the job," Dare said. "The folks are still upset by last night's trouble. I've got to make *them* forget. Reckon I'll have the boys pull off some Wild West stunt——"

Grant stopped. "You're going to bed," he said with the quiet authority that marked him a leader of men. "Leave the crowd to me."

"But I couldn't sleep! I'd just lie an' think——"

"Boy"—Grant's hand fell on his shoulder—"no good ever came of crying over spilt milk—or spilt blood, for that matter. From what Kit told me of the situation here, you only hastened the crisis. So don't get morbid, too. Go to bed—and sleep."

Dare obeyed. Finding an empty bunk, farthest from those his headstrong act had filled, he lay down, his thoughts drifting—— What damn lie was Jasper telling Allie now? Why hadn't he seen he was looting old graves? Where had Jim Grant learned horses —*Western* horses—like that?

Into his dreamless slumber cut the rumble of

wagons, the high-pitched voices of excited men, the tramp of feet, and Dare sprang up in his bunk to find the room filled with dusk and Perkins' cowboys, who had come to take their wounded home.

"What's the latest?" these eagerly demanded. "Any news?"

"Big news!" a burly buckaroo said grimly. "Sheriff Hardy's resigned!"

"The heck you say! Why?"

"He says he can't get no coöperation from Holt. Says the law won't protect his property, an' he's gotta resign an' protect it hisself. We met him out here—movin' the Three Star sheep up to join Cull Cole. Every road's full of woollies. Every herder's heeled. All you meet on the trails now is *ba-a-a, ba-a-a's,* an' dirty stares!"

"Who *is* sheriff?" Dare demanded hoarsely.

The fellow turned on him that same look of deference he had met in the eyes of every cowman encountered in Sundown that morning. "Nobody, Devlyn. They're lookin' for a man to pin Hardy's star on, but they'll have a long look. Every man's got too much on his hands now to want that job!" He did not see Dare recoil in dread, for, having saved his big news to the last, he swung back to address them all.

"Boys, history is sure repeatin' itself with a bang! They say Cull Cole's sent for 'Red' Madden's gang!"

And in the dead hush that fell on these words, every man in the room heard his own heart beating.

CHAPTER XIV

SWIFTLY the mighty current of time swept two weeks past, bringing nearer the hour when the seething fires of prejudice, so long restrained, would break forth. Ominously as the throb of a far-off tom-tom, these forces were felt the length and breadth of the Los Lobos range. Fierce-eyed old-timers, who had smoldered more years than Dare Devlyn had been a mortal, came from every nook and cranny, like old pumas from their lairs, to fight with the faction with whom their interests were aligned.

It was strange that these survivors of one black conflict were fiercest for another. They who had most cause to fear another range war, who had warned the younger generation against another, were, at its imminence, the irreconcilables! The fires of their hate, long banked and bedded with the coals of vengeance for property, friends, and kindred lost in the first outbreak, blazed to white heat with the fresh fuel of this.

But responsible sheepmen and cattlemen, shocked by the catastrophe impending, sought desperately to avert it. Cool heads among both factions appealed to Prosecutor Holt to stop it, and that official, regretting his first stand, made every possible effort to do so. But it was out of his hands. He could not placate ex-sheriff Hardy. He could not persuade any citizen to take Hardy's place. Nor could the county officials, convened to appoint a new sheriff, get a man to act. The range faced the supreme crisis of its existence with no help from the law. It seemed there was no help anywhere.

Cattlemen had been first in the Los Lobos. From the earliest days they had held undisputed sway there. When sheep first began to come in, there was no protest, for there was range for all. But, with sinister rapidity, the sheep increased. Greedy raisers overstocked the range, encroached on cattle range, and laid waste the land they ranged until, with passing years, the situation grew acute. Both sides faced financial ruin. The ever-increasing shortage of range, the violent, bitter prejudice of one group of men against the industry of the other, had culminated, thirty years ago, in one fierce outbreak, led by the Jessimers of Corral de Terra. Now, under worse pressure, it was to break out again, led, when the time came—both sides believed, because they wanted to believe—by the reckless youth who owned Corral de Terra and so stood in their eyes for the Jessimers. It was not the fault of one side or the other. It was the result of conditions. It was inevitable!

As Dare had unwittingly ignited the fire by unconsciously causing the first blood to be shed, so did the news that Cull Cole had hired Red Madden's gang to guard his sheep fan the flame beyond control. That crew of cutthroats were infamous on both sides of the border, and were always to be found where black trouble was afoot. If Cole had made this move in the hope of intimidating the cowmen, it failed miserably of having the intended effect. For the cowmen were roused into calling a council in

Sundown to adopt retaliatory measures in order to get even.

As a cattleman, Dare was forced to attend. And though, true to his promise to Kress, he said nothing, it was somehow voted as his measure that a great round-up be held and all Los Lobos cattle concentrated in one place for better protection. It was also voted as his measure that this place should be the very range in dispute—the land north of the Upper Rio. A strategic move! For with cowmen in possession of it, in occupancy of it, the sheepmen must be the invaders and bear the brunt of blame.

Little by little Dare was forced into the maelstrom, as other neutral cowmen were forced. He was compelled to send two men to represent Corral de Terra in the round-up. Sam, who was able to be in the saddle again, was one; and wild horses couldn't have kept Cim—despite the strange fascination Jim Grant still held for him—from being the other.

Men went from every ranch. And many outfits were left short-handed, necessitating the hiring of more men and those men—as the sheepmen direly noted—bore a better reputation for handling guns than for handling beef!

Soon the cattle hordes began to come down from the Nimbres to the west, and in from the Sulphur Desert to the east, and from horizon to horizon, north and south, to mingle and spread over the range that was the sheepmen's goal.

Standing in the door of his tent on the north bank of the Lower Rio, Cull Cole looked over the flat triangle of land between it and the Upper Rio, an island made by the river forks. Sheep crowded it—thousands upon thousands of sheep. Los Lobos

sheepmen, faced with the necessity of obtaining grass
or losing their flocks, had rallied about him to a
man. But the feed in this limited area was going
fast, would, in a week, be gone!

Shading his eyes from the sun glare with a brown,
veined hand, the old sheepman looked across the
north fork of the Rio to the disputed range. He
saw the cattle herds assembling, guarded by hostile
riders from every outfit in that country, as vigilantly
as Red Madden's ruffians guarded the concentrated
sheep. He saw the grass up there—so plentiful, so
near. And that grass mocked him!

"Cull," said Joe Philips to his friend and neighbor
in a voice tremulous with the consciousness of terrible peril, "this thing comin'—it's too much, Cull,
for a man to have on his soul! Let's turn back."

"To what?" Cole's dark-skinned face blazed with
wrath, his long body seemed to lift and strain with
it. "To the dust heap we left behind? To sure
ruination? Joe, I've been losin' hundreds of dollars
every day because of poor grass. The only grass left
is ahead. Look at it—goin' to waste! We was
allotted this North o' Rio range——"

"Because Corral de Terra was wrecked!" broke in
Philips. "Because it was deserted, an' had no herd
to need it! If Corral de Terra had been in operation,
this range would not have been allotted to us, Cull.
It's their range by right. With it runnin' again,
you know, Cull, that ol' pact wouldn't stand."

"I know"—Cole's jaw set like a rock—"that it
was a black day for us when Devlyn—curse him!—
brought Corral de Terra back. It would be a blessin'
to sheepmen if it was wrecked again. But as things
stand, that range is ours, an' we're goin' to take it!"

As resolute was Gid Perkins, camped on the Upper Rio, in full view of Cole's camp, maddened by sight, scent, and sound of the animals he hated.

"Renege—*now?*" he blazed, with the driven intensity that had worried Kit Kress months ago. "Turn this country over to sheep? Be in their fix in a year? No! With Corral de Terra back, that ol' truce don't stand. We're goin' to settle this once an' for all— take the Los Lobos for beef! We've held in long enough—*too* long. Now, by gravy, I'm goin' to fight for what's mine—like a man!"

So they waited—the cowmen for the first sheep to be driven across the Upper Rio ford, the sheepmen for the opportune time. But the wait could not be long, for daily the grass on that flat triangle vanished. There was nothing to return to. They had no recourse but to go on. And in the interval of waiting, both factions—as nations, in the midst of peace, prepare for war—made ready. Both had some far-fetched hope of an eleventh-hour compromise. But, as nations view the militant signs that mock peace talk, so did each side view the other's preparations as a challenge and threat.

In the meanwhile, Corral de Terra pursued the uneven tenor of its way. Hardly an hour passed but some dark rumor reached it. Unknown cowboys had fired on Grouse Creek herders. A man had ordered mutton in a Sundown restaurant, thereby starting a rough-house that wrecked the place. A cowboy had died in his boots in a Cache Valley skirmish. So common were these reports that they made small impression. A danger ever present is a danger ignored.

To most of Dare's guests, familiar only with a

decorous, organized existence, the situation was fantastic. One broke the law—one was jailed. Such was their simple rule of order. They could not comprehend that this country had not altered in thought or precept from the old days, old ways; that it was lost to an always indifferent world by its natural barriers and its very immensity. They did not believe the issue would ever come to pass, and they made the most of their holiday, as, in cities reared in the shadow of a smoking volcano, the heedless citizenry feast and dance.

Dare, racking his brain to devise ways and means of entertaining the guests, had his own mind deadened to the crisis. He staged bucking contests so frequently that the horses grew dog-gentle. The steers used for bulldogging became so canny that when they saw a cowboy coming toward them they would beat him to it and lie down. Rope spinning, trick riding, and horse races lost their novelty. Riding lessons palled. And then excursions were arranged to the hills—hunting, fishing, hiking—always with careful avoidance of the river forks that promised to be the battle ground.

On all these trips, Dare was Madge Grant's escort. Eloise, who had transferred her heart interest in Dare to Mace, once confided to the latter—as they sauntered about—that enamored cowboy with the kodak "shooting her," as the cowboys expressed it, "all over the place"—that Dare Devlyn "simply worships the ground that Madge walks on!" It was no exaggeration.

If Allie had dimmed the glory of Madge's hair for Dare, if he could never look at it without the vague suspicion that it was the work of artifice and not nature—a suspicion absolutely unfounded, but irremovable, for such is the power of suggestion— there was still sufficient luster about the Eastern girl to dazzle him completely. He worshiped her still—as a divinity, almost, and as remote from him as one.

His quarrel with Allie had troubled him for days. He felt that he ought to apologize—he did not know for what—but she had forbidden him to speak to her. And, though he did so whenever chance afforded, she gave him so few chances, so plainly wished him not to, that, hurt and resentful, he gave up, and devoted himself entirely to Madge.

What Jim Grant thought of this was what Mrs. Mills, particularly, wanted to know. But Grant gave no sign. He took no part in the activities. Occasionally he drove to Sundown for a visit with Kit Kress, but for the most part he stayed close to the ranch. And many times each day Dare ran across him, seated on the bench beneath the sycamores, staring out over the court, or up at El Capitan, buried deep in thought. Perhaps thinking the thoughts he had at sixty, Dare would guess then, which he would not have had, had he done more thinking at twenty-two.

What Allie thought of Dare's infatuation, nobody ever wondered or cared. If she was unhappy, nobody knew. If her pillow was wet with tears each night, the canvas walls of the *Santa Maria* hid it. And she must have cried into it very softly, for even Swap, sleeping in the tent hard by, did not hear. Dare never saw her otherwise than laughing—usually with Jasper Kade.

She had a smile for every one but Madge and

himself.   She made no secret of her dislike for Madge.   Dare could not understand that.

She was no longer the shy, wild girl he had found in the melancholy ruins of Corral de Terra.   Her whole disposition had undergone a change.   She neither shunned nor courted the visitors, to whom her history made her a romantic figure.   And she was a great favorite with all.

This new Allie seemed to glory in the very things that had once pained and shamed her.   She insisted on being called "Albuquerque" in full.   She would convulse them by tales of Swap's tricky deals.   She even told them of her encounter with Mrs. Hutchins. And she seemed to delight in wearing the oldest rags she had, especially she clung to the patched and tattered little blue overalls.   Yet, withal, she was so vivid, so unquenchable, that none noticed what she wore.   No one, that is, but Madge, and she only in the kindest spirit.

"She's a beauty!" Madge once enthused to Dare. "I'm wild to see her dressed up!   She'd be stunning. Did you know I even schemed for that pleasure? My rose crêpe gown—it would just suit her.   I knew she wouldn't take it from me, so I gave it to Mrs. Mills to give her in return for some favor Allie had done for her.   Mrs. Mills said her eyes lighted like a child's on seeing its first Christmas tree, but she declined it with thanks."

"Allie didn't use to be like this!" Dare protested. "I don't know what's got into her."

Madge gave him the queerest look then.   "Don't you?" she softly asked.

"Not unless it's Jasper Kade's influence," said the boy.   "I'd sure admire to wring that yahoo's neck!"

A healthy contempt for Jasper was one of the many sentiments that Madge and Dare Devlyn shared.

As for Swap Boone—that itinerant trader was in the seventh heaven. Whether he had inherited his social graces from Grandpop Hez Boone, of Hickory Springs, Arkansas, or, indeed, from the illustrious Daniel, the fact remains that he was, for the first time in his ilfe, a social success.

Discovering his talent for telling stories, the Corral de Terra guests clamored for them. And in the first few days, he spent hours in the dim, old hall that no sun, no number of lamps, could really brighten, reciting tales that made them shiver. He filled the listeners with delicious apprehension just by his tone.

Not tales of Corral de Terra did he tell now, but of the personage uppermost in Los Lobos minds. Tingling, truthful tales Swap told of one whose deeds beggared imagination, of a person Swap had met in his years of continual perambulation, back and forth and crisscross through the great Southwest, of the renegade—Red Madden!

A name to scare children with, Swap told them. "Be good, or Red Madden'll git you!" they said to frightened border kids. "Many a full-grown man had heard it an' never looked the same!" declared the old trader to his interested listeners.

Dread and sinister, Swap painted him, and truly. And his audience, hearing, would clap for more, and say how "perfectly thrilling" it would be to meet him. For Red Madden was only a name to them —as yet!

CHAPTER XV

"DARE, YOU'RE BLIND."

DESPITE his popularity with the guests, Swap was not one to put pleasure ahead of business, and his business was trading. As he confided to Dare, "being a social lion buttered no parsnips."

When he had pulled out so summarily, leaving Dare to reconstruct Corral de Terra, Swap had killed two birds with one stone: Avoided work, abhorrent to his nature, and taken the opportunity to exchange the heterogeneous contents of the old prairie schooner for articles more to a dude's fancy—Navajo blankets, Indian moccasins, Mexican jewelry, mounted antlers, and the like.

But, to his chagrin, none of Dare's dudes fancied them, and his inability to trade with them preyed on his mind. He was more down in the mouth than Allie had ever seen him until, utterly without warning, the tide of luck turned his way. And, thereafter, he snapped his suspenders so frequently in the line of business that they lost their elasaticity and he had to take up the slack.

It came about one fine morning when Mrs. Mills chanced to take her constitutional along the river bank. Swap—inspired, surely, for he stood in no little awe of this dignified lady from Schenectary—inveigled her into camp, and reverently unwrapped and demonstrated his white elephant, the cuckoo clock, magnanimously offering to trade it for one of the rings that adorned her fingers. But both Swap's persuasive voice and the vocal efforts of the mangy little bird that inhabited the clock left Mrs. Mills cold. In fact, much of the eloquence of both were lost on her. For her interest—as Swap saw to his disgust—was on a vase of wild flowers that Allie had placed on a near-by stump. Turning, as though to go, she paused to examine the vase. Carefully avoiding Swap's eye, she said, with an indifference that would have done credit to the trader himself:

"I'll trade the topaz ring for this vawz."

"The—which?" Swap stared at her blankly.

"This vawz." Suppressed desire clipped the lady's speech even more short than usual. "Will you trade?"

"Great Goliath, yeah!" Swap was too stunned to dicker. "But—I thought it was a *vase!*"

And he thought she was crazy, trading this valuable ring for that old doodad that Allie had picked up somewhere, and that had been kicking around camp longer than he could remember. Why, it wasn't even trading timber! Nothing—just an old vase— *"vawz,"* she called it. What if a vawz—— With a sneaking fear that *he* might be the crazy one, Swap looked up to see Ezra Biggers puffing into camp.

"I say, Boone," Ezra panted, mopping his face, "have you any more of that pre-American stuff?"

Swap batted his eyes. "That—*which?*"

"Anything more like that exquisite bit of pottery you traded Mrs. Mills? Why, it's glorious! A rare find. Out of an Aztec temple—possibly even Toltec! Have you any more old relics like that?"

Hiding his chagrin at having been worsted by a

tenderfoot, Swap said he had. And in the hope that springs eternal, he unswaddled the cuckoo for Biggers, who turned from it with a snort of disgust.

But a trail had been blazed to Swap's camp, and it became part of the regular routine to sit about his camp fire and clash wits with him. The very things the guests had scorned to buy had a new value when they could bargain for them. The genial manner in which Swap conducted the business—his genuine good-nature, and amusing monologues—made it all huge fun. Now and then some one struck a real find, as Mrs. Mills had done; but they would dicker as seriously for some worthless object as though the deal involved millions. And Mrs. Mills became so adept in the art, took to it "so natural," that Swap —without the slightest trace of professional jealousy —constantly encouraged her to "git a wagon, an' take to the road."

The trading mania spread even among the guests themselves, so that there was no telling one day in whose possession a piece of portable property would be the next. And if the canny old trader most often came out the big end of the horn, who cared? The game was the thing. But most of the deals were as unprofitable as they were involved. Like this one, for instance:

Las Vegas, who was convalescent now, and very much a part of the fun, had a gorgeous bandanna that Eloise craved. Swap knew of this; also he knew that Las Vegas had a sweetheart over on Grouse Creek—and he had heard the puncher remark that she had a birthday coming and he was up a tree what to give her. That was sufficient to set Swap's wits to work.

Recently, Mrs. Mills had offered him a manicure set in a trade that had not gone through because Swap would not give boot.

"Boot," he had told her more than once, "is the science of tradin'. Remember to allus git boot, an' don't give it, an' you'll be a success." And Mrs. Mills remembered.

Now, that manicure set was the very thing for Las Vegas' girl. So Swap sought for ways to get it. Yesterday, he had traded Eloise a pair of beaded moccasins that Mrs. Mills admired. Working on these premises, he snapped his galluses and waded in.

After much dickering, Eloise traded the moccasins and a fountain pen for a hammered silver ring, set with a Mexican turquoise. Then Swap endeavored to trade the moccasins to Mrs. Mills for the manicure set, "even up." But his brilliant pupil insisted on boot. So Swap made a deal on the side. Under the plea that he was "danged nigh dead for a whittle," he borrowed Ezra Biggers' knife. And how he went after it! It was too light for a he-man; it was a lady's knife, Swap declared. What would Biggers do if he was to meet a "hicklesnifter" on one of these wild trails and had to defend himself with that knife? And so on and on, until Biggers, disgusted with his property, swapped it for the fountain pen Eloise had given in boot.

Then ensued a session of frenzied finance between Swap and Mrs. Mills, over the moccasins and the manicure set, such as Wall Street seldom witnessed. The wily old trader and the canny society woman had it nip and tuck, until Swap played his hole card by throwing in Biggers' knife as boot—a deal the lady was quick to snap up.

Then Swap traded the manicure set to Las Vegas for the bandanna and two strings of lace leather—which last he sold for two bits to a cowboy who happened to need them for saddle strings—traded the bandanna to Eloise for the turquoise ring, and emerged from a hard day's work with his original property, two bits in cash, and much satisfaction.

However, this was only a side line with Swap. First and last he was a horse trader. While absent, he had traded off most of the old wrecks of which he had been possessed when Dare first met him, and had acquired several fairly presentable saddle ponies. And so well had Swap anticipated Dare's needs that the lot were purchased eventually, greatly swelling the old wallet he had offered Allie. This left him with four dilapidated plugs, which he described as "swappin' stock," and he made frequent journeys to Sundown, to ease his "foot-ich" and trade horses. Though he exchanged them a dozen times, no one would have guessed it, for each lot was as decrepit as the original four.

But by no hook or crook, at home or abroad, could he "work off" the cuckoo clock. It remained on his hands and weighed heavily on his spirits, shaking his confidence in his trading ability until he became so low in his mind that he was haunted by thoughts of a dark day coming, when he might have to "put down a root" like less gifted folks and take a "job of work."

So, with trading, hiking, riding, and nightly dances in the vast old hall, the sands of the fateful days ran out, bringing the eve of the day before the entire party would leave for Devil's Gorge. This jaunt had been planned as the biggest event of the season.

The spot chosen was the wildest, loneliest, in all the Nimbres—a spot so wildly grand that it was as if Nature had reserved one place to which she might retire to refresh herself by viewing her own handiwork, unspoiled by man. The party were going in the wagon, together with blankets, provisions, and other camp gear, for they planned to stay three days.

This last night before starting, Dare and Madge sat out on the gallery. A full, white moon looked into the court, and it gave the girl a breath-taking, ethereal beauty that seemed to set her farther apart from Dare. And there was both pain and ecstasy in his heart, as, accompanying himself on Las Vegas' guitar, he taught her to sing "My Little Ol' Sod Shanty on the Plains."

But, ever and anon, his gaze would stray to Allie and Jasper Kade, dim on the bench under the sycamores. And, seeing Jasper's eyes devour the girl, his hand close possessively on hers, Dare's own fingers made a sharp discord.

"The Lost Chord!" Madge laughingly declared, noting the cause. And to cover his confusion, she took the guitar, and thrummed softly for a while. Then, in a sweet, cultivated voice, she began to sing, in harmony with the witchery of the night and the sad, old setting:

"When in thy dreaming
  Moons like these shall shine again,
And daylight beaming
  Prove thy dreams are vain——"

Carried completely out of himself by the glamour of the night, her voice, her nearness to him, the cowboy said tensely:

"No moon will ever shine like this again! An' no daybreak can prove anything. For I know it now—that my dream is vain!"

Her eyes held his in the perfumed, pulsing silence. "Dare," she said sharply, "you're blind!"

In husky apology, he told her, "Love *is* blind!"

She saw that he misunderstood her, but let it pass. And after a long moment in which she studied his face—so young, so earnest, so good to look upon— she looked away, saying gently: "Have you asked Allie to go to Devil's Gorge with us?"

He had not—having had no chance. But it was understood that she was going. Dare knew she was —for he had overheard her and Jasper planning on the trip.

"Little she cares"—his voice was strangely husky —"for an invite from me!"

They were late getting away the next morning, and the heat of the day was upon them before the wagon was hitched. While this was in progress, with every one rushing out of the house with loaded arms, and in again like ants in an overturned hill, old Cim galloped in.

It was Dare's first glimpse of Cim since he had left to aid in the round-up, for he had remained at the ford with Corral de Terra's herd. The sight of him sharply recalled the dread situation. Days of dwelling with old passions, of digging up old memories, had swept the foreman to the high crest of the newly surging tide. The wisdom of thirty years had been cast off as shackles; the spirit of earlier years flared in his eyes.

"They're due to break pronto!" he flung at Dare. "The sheep's starved out. That flat between the rivers is eat to dust. We look for 'em to make a break in the night. Son, they've got some mean fighters back of 'em. We're goin' to need all the help we can rustle. You'll benefit most, if that North o' Rio range is saved for beef, so git up there an' help. Take every man you can. Cowmen's lookin' to you—to the ol' brand—to lead!"

Suddenly, in every throbbing vein of him, Dare wanted to go—felt he ought to go—*would* go!

"I'm goin'!" he cried to Grant, as Cim rode off, completely carried away by the recklessness so long repressed. "I won't skulk like a coyote no longer! I brought this on. It can't be helped now. I'm not goin' to let other people fight for my range."

"You're going to look after these people you brought here!" contradicted Grant sharply. "When this breaks, Corral de Terra will be a mighty dangerous place. Take them up to Devil's Gorge as you planned. Keep them there till I send word!"

What was it that cooled Dare's blood, bent his hot will into instant obedience to this rich promoter from Maine? Surely, some Heaven-sent prescience of the amazing truth, not fully realized by himself as yet.

"I'm goin' into town now," Grant said, more calmly, "riding in with Swap Boone. But, thereafter, I'll be at the ranch—all the time. Take good care of Madge."

As he spoke, the covered wagon lumbered into the court, hitched to the two most decrepit of the superannuated four—if there could be any choice. And there was Allie, perched on the high seat beside Swap.

Even before the rig stopped for Grant, Jasper was leaning over the wheel on Allie's side, commanding, arguing, and finally, pleading, with her to get down and go on the picnic, as she had promised. But Allie refused steadfastly. Dare, ignoring Jasper utterly, went up to her.

"Allie," he begged, "come along with us."

Jasper turned on him with a sneer. "Save your breath, buster! If she won't go for me, she won't for you!"

In a sudden, inexplicable flare of anger, "Who the heck are *you?*" Dare demanded, shouldering him roughly aside, as though he were the nonentity his tone implied.

"Of course you'll go, Allie?"

"No," she said listlessly, "I'm goin' to town with pop."

Dare was shocked by this close view of her face. It was so small, somehow, compared to her eyes, or her eyes were so big—he didn't know which. Her eyes were so black, and her face so white——

"Allie"—always he thanked Heaven that here, at this last moment of fateful parting, he made that plea—"Allie, let's bury the hatchet. Let's don't be mad any more. Come, Allie—let's be friends!"

"It ain't that, Dare." Her wistful smile wrung his heart as it had of yore. "It ain't just meanness in me, but——"

"Wimmin's romantical," joked Swap, with a broad wink at Dare. "This is Saturday, savvy? She might see Red Madden in town."

And another grim truth was spoken in jest!

CHAPTER XVI

"I'LL WRECK IT AGAIN!"

IN ordinary times, Sundown would have slept through this day of stifling heat. A half dozen ponies would have drowsed in the streets, dogs would have napped in the doorways, and a mere handful of ranchers droned in the shade. But this was no ordinary time, and the little cow town was wary and wide awake.

Again, as on that day when Dare had rushed in with every hope of preventing the crisis at hand, Sundown was jammed with armed, grim men. But with this difference—not all were cowmen now. Sheepmen in equal proportion were here, transacting Saturday business, getting supplies for their combined camp. Both factions went steadily about their own affairs, neither giving nor taking an inch. For they walked in full knowledge that it was a smoking volcano they trod, that the terrible issue might come at any time—to-night, perhaps, and the most implacable of them cared not to hasten it, or precipitate it, and have that black weight on his soul.

Only when friends or neighbors of long standing met was the feud even discussed, and then only in whispers. Hard to tell enemy, now, from friend, for more strangers had been hired by both sides than could be kept track of, and hirelings from both sides were here. And both sides hated these hirelings, far more bitterly than they hated each other. Cowmen, meeting heavily gunned, swaggering riders at every turn—recognized by some as Red Madden's gang—had their restraint put to the test.

Into this charged atmosphere rolled the *Santa Maria* just before noon.

"Drop me off at Kit's office," Grant requested as they neared it. "I'll be around handy, when it's time to go home."

"Take your time." Swap was jocose, in spite of the heat. "I hope to scare up a trade or two. An' a hombre kin allus go home, when he ain't no place else to go."

They let Grant off, and Swap tickled the derelicts into a resumption of action. His eyes raked the sidewalks, as he drove on to the far end of town to leave the rig.

"I wisht you'd 'a' gone on the picnic, baby," he fretted to Allie. "I'll hate leavin' you—with all these hoodlums in town.

"I'll be all right," she smiled wanly. Swap did not know that she could not go, could not accept Dare's hospitality. She was too tired to go, too tired of making believe she loved Jasper—when Dare did not care, too tired to stay mad at Dare, to hate Madge, like she ought to. Maybe she ought not to hate Madge now, reflected poor little Allie. She had thought Madge was just flirting with Dare—but she wasn't. Allie had heard them talking last night, and had heard Dare tell Madge that his dream was vain. And Madge told him he was blind—blind to think it was vain! Well, Madge would open his eyes on the picnic, and she could not bear seeing that.

"A full house," remarked Swap, turning into the

vacant lot reserved for wagons and ponies, and now full of both. But he found room for the *Santa Maria* near the long tie rack, unhitched the derelicts, watered them at the trough, and tied them to the wheel—just for looks, for they'd have stood until doomsday without being tied. Then they ate the lunch Allie had brought, and Swap drifted away, scouting out prospects in the crowd, while Allie crawled back on the high wagon seat, looking drearily on.

Men flowed by in a stream. Some of them turned to stare at her brazenly. She shrank back, making herself as inconspicuous as possible, embarrassed to note that she was the one woman here. With trouble afoot, Los Lobos ranchers had left their women at home.

"Hot!" a passing voice complained.

"Too danged hot," affirmed another. "A storm's brewin', Dave. Sure be a good one when it comes —held off so long."

"Waal, we'll feel all the better for it. Clear the air, Sam."

An hour later Swap came back, and found Allie still sitting up there.

"I thought you'd be skylarkin' uptown!" he exclaimed. "Lookin' at the gimcracks in the winders. Usually I hafta drag you——"

"I'm just goin', pop."

She saw that he was worried about her.

But the windows held little lure. There were three dry-goods stores in Sundown, and she played no favorites, visiting each in turn. Once she would have spent hours before each window display—dreaming she owned every dress there, dreaming she was a fine

lady going to parties and places, wearing them all.
But now—— She didn't care about being a lady,
didn't care about clothes. All she saw in the windows now was herself mirrored back—in her red
calico dress, faded from many washings, dusty and
rumpled from the trip—herself, and a mental picture
of Madge, as she had looked that morning, so dainty
and sweet, in the rose crêpe sports frock she had
worn to the gorge.

Turning sharply from the pictures that tortured,
Allie saw that she was right across the street from
Kit Kress' office. Kit's buckboard stood out in front,
and, as she watched, the agent and Jim Grant came
out, got in the rig, and drove off. Dully, she hoped
that Grant would not be gone long, that they could
go home soon, for her head ached—from the heat.

To get out of it, she went back to the *Santa Maria*.
Swap was not there. No telling when he would be.
Allie had learned long ago not to look for him till
she saw him coming; half her life had been spent
in this old wagon, waiting for Swap.

She crept over the seat and curled up like a kitten
on her bed, spread on the wagon box. Oh, it was
hot! It *was* going to storm, for that was thunder
muttering off to the west. She hoped Swap would
come before the storm broke. She was afraid of
thunder. He always laughed at that and told her
thunder never hurt any one yet. But it hurt now
—hurt her head. She hoped Dare would not be out
in it, hoped Madge would get wet——

She slept. And in her sleep—Allie's only escape
now from wretched realities, having forsworn waking
dreams—she was with Dare among the lupines of
the old court. Madge had never been there. Yet,

in the cool of sunset, he was looking at her, as he did at Madge, asking her what she would do if her dreams came true. And she told him she would buy Corral de Terra, fix it up, take the curse off it——

"I'll wreck it again!" he swore, and his voice was ugly, and he was ugly, like a picture she had seen of the devil once! And she was scared to death of him——

Then, hideously, Allie knew that that voice wasn't Dare's, that she wasn't asleep—but sitting bolt upright in the hot wagon, fighting back screams, holding her heart firmly with both hands to keep it from jumping right out of her berast.

"We've corralled enough powder to do it right," said the ugly voice, just outside the canvas partition. "We'll wreck it a blamed sight worse than it was before!"

"Ain't that goin' far—even for you, Red?" A second rough voice reached the shuddering girl. "The law——"

Red Madden laughed coarsely. "I ain't seen any in this neck of the woods myself! But you're right, 'Mustang,' in a way. This can't go on. After the big fight's pulled off, the soldiers'll come. An' when they do, we're up the flume. Our necks'll be in the halter, sure! What's yours worth—to *you?* The ten bucks a day we're gittin' for this? Seventy more, for the week it'll last? Mine's worth a heap more to me! An' I ain't riskin' it for a good many times that. We can ask our own price for the girl——"

"That part's jake." With every strung nerve Allie was listening. "But Corral de Terra—even Cull Cole won't stand for that!"

Madden swore viciously. "No! Neither would

he stand for our takin' the girl! But what he don't know won't hurt him! It's to his interests to have the place wrecked like it was before—for that'll dispose of the cowmen's claim on that range. They ain't got the nerve to do it! Besides, we're here to do their dirty work. What he wants of us is to stop lead when the fight comes off to-night—while they cross the sheep. But I don't aim to be slaughtered that a way! I'm a man of my word, an' I'll do what I said I would when I took the job—put the sheep north of Rio. It's nobody's business *how* I do it, an' it's nobody's business if we pull off this big job for ourselves on the side, an' rake in some real coin!"

"How much does Cull know?" asked the man called Mustang.

"Nothin'! I told him I had a scheme—that's all. I told him to start the sheep across at dark—that I saw a way to git 'em over, an' keep 'em there. I told him to ask me no questions, an' I'd tell him no lies."

Their voices dropped, fell almost under the rumbling thunder, yet the straining girl heard.

"We pull out pronto," Madden was saying. "I told the gang to wait for us at Willow Springs—the road forks off there for Devil's Gorge. I'll take four men, beat it up there, an' nab Devlyn an' the Grant girl. You wait at the springs. I don't look for much trouble at that end, for Devlyn's just got one cowboy with him, and them dudes——"

"Devlyn's liable to give you a handful. I'd size him up as one bad hombre!"

Madden laughed again, with a significance that froze Allie's blood. "He'll git no chance! We'll

have the drop on him. If he fights later—— Well,
dead men's easy handled! But if he's docile, we'll
turn him loose when the sheep are over, on his agreement to make the cowmen let them stay there. We'll
have the girl in our hands, an' we can make him
perform. He's sweet on her, savvy? Besides, it
ain't goin' to hurt the sheepmen none if Dare Devlyn
—the cattle leader—is plumb eliminated! Now, when
I git back to the springs with 'em, we'll all go on to
the ranch, an' tend to that. It'll be a cinch, too, for
there's only a handful of men out there. We'll plant
that powder where it'll do the most good, an' set it
off just before dark.

"In the meantime"—Allie fought the faintness of
horror to catch it—"we send word to the cowmen
guardin' the ford that Corral de Terra is under attack. They'll leave everything an' ramp down there
—too late. While they're out of the way, the herders
cross the sheep. There won't be a shot fired! Pretty
slick, if I do say it! Then, with the sheep north
of Rio, an' the key ranch put back where it was before—it will stay that way, too, for Devlyn will go
bust along with it, an' nobody else would have it on
a bet—that cleans up our job here in one grand
sweep. They we're gone—with the girl. We can
raise the ante as high as we please, for her dad's
a big mogul back East. An' when he buys her back,
we can live in clover the rest of our——"

Wind whipped up the old wagon-sheet. Thunder
boomed louder. Allie was frantic. Had they gone?
She did not dare look. Ages she waited, scarce daring to breath. Then, in a lull of the rising storm,
she heard the scuffle of a boot heel on the gravel,
the scratch of a match, and the two voices discussing

the devilish plot—to steal Madge, "eliminate" Dare if he fought, and wreck the old ranch. Then there were ages when she could not hear, and the wind almost whipped the cover of the *Santa Maria* from over her head. A dozen times she was on the point of jumping out and running for help. Then she would hear the voices again, and thank Heaven she had been quiet. She prayed that the men would go, so she could leave. Then she took her prayers back—for when the men went, they would surely be going to start the trouble.

And when, at awful length, she heard them mount and ride off, Allie went crazy. She jumped out of the wagon and ran up and down, distractedly crying, "Pop! Pop!" But the lot was deserted—which was why Red Madden and Mustang had deemed it safe to retire to it for conference. Lightning played continually in the west. The storm would be a good one when it came, and most of the ranchers were beating it home.

Up the street Allie ran, in her frenzy, seeking her father, in too much terror of strangers, now, to inquire of the few men she met. She saw no one she knew—no one she could trust. Vainly she sought Swap the full length of the street.

Where was Jim Grant? Not back at Kit's office! For when with frantic hands she beat on Kit's door, a face leered into hers.

"The agent's out, sis," a rough voice mocked. "Won't I do as well?"

With a moan of despair she whirled and fought the high wind back to the wagon. Maybe Swap would be there now. He would not let them blow up the old house! He knew how she loved it. The

old house that had always been open to her—every
window and door—when no other house was.   She
had made mud pies in the court, when she was a
baby, and, growing up, played it was home.   She had
met Dare there.   They were going to kill Dare!   For
that's what it meant!   He'd fight—he'd *die*—to keep
Madge out of their hands!   They would kill Dare
—who had been good to her when nobody else was!

The fact that Corral de Terra was doomed, that
Madge Grant was to be stolen for ransom by the
most villainous crew in the whole Southwest, was
nothing compared to the terrible fact that Red Madden was on his way *now* to kill Dare!   Some one
must beat him up there.   She must—for Swap had
not come back!

Running to the team, Allie was unhitching the first
old wreck when she stopped, her heart all but stop-
ping, too, at the thought.   This horse was so stiff,
old, and slow!   It could not make it to Devil's Gorge
in time—in *any* time!   And already men on fast
horses were gone!

CHAPTER XVII

"JESSIMER'S BACK!"

WILDLY Allie looked about. As if in answer to her heart's wild appeal, a star-faced sorrel came down the street. In the saddle was a vacant-eyed, round-faced youth, whom she dimly recalled having seen before—when the *Santa Maria* had stopped at his father's dry-land farm on the edge of the Los Lobos range to trade. Swap had said he was a "clodhopper; didn't know beans." That memory merely flickered through Allie's mind, for her whole strung, quivering being was bent on his horse —a wiry, long-limbed, racy sorrel. She must get it! Dare's life might depend upon it! But how?

Allie—daughter of the itinerant trader, Swap Boone—knew but one way to get it. Everything she had ever owned, Swap had obtained in just that way. But Swap was not here to get it for her——

Fighting down her terror for Dare, her mad need for haste, she waved at the rider, Swap's invariable greeting springing spontaneously to her lips:

"Howdy, stranger! How's tricks?"

The boy drew up, open-mouthed. His mind having mastered the fact that this pretty girl was accosting him, he reined in and, grinning foolishly, rode onto the lot.

Concealing her panic as best she could, Allie walked about the sorrel, ran a hand over it. "Right smart pony—that!" Her voice was persuasive, her eye hypnotic—the voice and eye of Swap!

"Yah," agreed the owner, almost falling off it in his surprise.

"Still"—Allie, the born actress, with many years' observation of this rôle, teetered back—one could almost have heard a suspender snap—and reflected aloud—"still, it ain't much good for a farm. Too light, too fast, for a plow. No bottom. Nope! Not a farmer's horse—a-tall! The horse you need is that bay, yonder. How'll you swap?"

The boy's mouth opened to its amazing limit. "Nuthin' doin'," he grinned—not having it in his heart to laugh right out at her—such a cute little thing!

"Take another look, stranger!"—dear Heaven, make him trade!—"That bay's worth a couple of dozen of it—on a ranch. Gentle as a kitten. Eats less than a burro. True as steel. Will stick to a furrow all day if you ask it. Thin, now, I'll allow —but it'll fill out when it's put to grass. If you're half as smart as I take you for, you'll trade!"

That put the boy in a bad box. He did not want to spoil her good opinion of him. Neither did he want to trade his horse.

"Now!" he said, and with a flip of the reins, was about to ride away from temptation when she cried, in the inspiration born of despair:

"Wait here a minnit!" Her black eyes were mesmeric. *"Please,* wait!"

"Yah." He would do that—anything but trade.

And he waited, while she scrambled into the old prairie schooner and came back, bringing something in her arms. Kneeling in the dirt, bidding him dismount and kneel also, she unwrapped the article, with all Swap's reverent touch.

Inspired himself, the boy said brilliantly, "Clock!"

"You'd be surprised," Allie came back, with a lightness that cost her much.

With shaking fingers, she wound the old relic, turning the hands to within a few seconds of one. Yet it seemed an eternity before the little bird popped out in the face of the dumfounded youth, *cuckooing* once.

The boy's face beamed like a full moon. "Golly!" he breathed. "Can it do it again?"

"Every hour!" Swap's daughter assured him. And, steeling herself to waste time that she might make it, she set the hands at twelve to give the cuckoo all the chance in the world to speak for itself. And to the rumble of thunder and lightning flash, it sang to the end its changeless song.

And the boy said "Golly!" again.

"The bay, *an' the cuckoo to boot,* for your pony!" pleaded the girl. "Trade, an' you'll see the little bird every hour of your life, if you give Methuselah aces an' spades!" Which was true, if he'd wind it every hour! An all but overpowering faintness came over her as he recklessly vowed:

"By golly, I trade!"

While the boy uncinched the saddle, Allie jerked the bridle off, and snatching up the tie rope, looped it around the sorrel's neck, threw a half-hitch over its nose, and then, while he stood with mouth agape and eyes agog, she leaped on bareback and tore breathlessly down the street.

She rode so wildly that, when she passed a rider on a roan horse coming in, head bent to the wind, she was a half block farther before it dawned on her that he looked like Cim. But she could not risk waiting time to go back and make sure. And when, on the outskirts of town, she sighted some one she knew, some one she could trust, and tried to stop, pulling on the rope with all her might, throwing back against it all her inadequate weight, she could not slow the mettlesome horse until she was twenty yards past. Then, too jealous of those yards toward Dare to return, she screamed, "Pop! Pop!"

Swap Boone, who had turned to admire the horse, froze in his tracks .

"Pop"—she had not time for it all, dare not risk muddling him with more—"they're crossin' the sheep to-night! I heard Red Madden talkin'! He's on his way to the gorge—to kill Dare—to steal Madge Grant! He's goin' to dynamite Corral de Terra at dark! You stop 'em, pop!"

"Baby," yelled Swap, "where in blue blazes did you git that hoss?"

She was far from him then, and only one word conquered the distance—"Cuckoo!"

Swap was dazed. It was moments before another thought could enter his brain. Meanwhile, he traversed the town, and came to the vacant lot.

There, bellying up in the wind, was the *Santa Maria*. Tied to the wheel, one old plug was lonesomely nickering to its mate, which a moon-faced youth, bearing a bundle of familiar shape, was leading off.

"Hey, that's my hoss!" yelled Swap.

"Naw," denied the satisfied customer. "I traded the girl my pony for it."

"An' what?" asked Swap huskily.

"You'd be surprised! *A cuckoo clock!*"

Then it was true! The old trader's heart swelled, and his head, too. *His* girl had done that! Metaphorically, he patted himself on the back. Allie was a chip of the old block! Deliriously, he called after the boy: *"I'm her pop!"*

That seemed to release the pressure upon Swap's brain, for other thoughts flew through it—other, awful thoughts! Allie—his baby—was racing Red Madden to Devil's Gorge! She was in mortal danger! She would be caught in the storm. And she was afraid of thunderstorms, always hid in the darkest place she could find, covered her head, and came out looking like she'd been through a sick spell—so white——

Swap started after her, down the street, crying distractedly, "Allie! Allie!" as she had cried to him. Then he remember that she had said Madden's ruffians were going to dynamite the old ranch, and his brain rang to the echo of her trustful: "You stop 'em, pop!" And he stretched his long legs as they had never been stretched, in that run uptown. People stared after him, came after him, thinking it was bad news from the headquarters up on the Rio that he brought. But, heedless of their demands, Swap ran on.

Kit's buckboard was just drawing up in front of the office. Kit and Jim Grant were in it. And, to his boundless relief, Swap saw old Cim reining up beside Grant. With a last burst of speed, he reached the wheel, and, puffing like an engine, he gasped:

"Red Madden—dynamite—Corral de Terra——"

The crowd that had followed closed in, clamoring

over the clamorous thunder. How? When? Where?
How did he know?

"My gal overheard 'em!" Swap jerked out. "They
ain't done it yet, but they're goin' to at dark—Red
Madden's men! Madden's on his way to the gorge
right now—to kill Devlyn—an' run off with your
daughter, Grant! My gal's gone to warn 'em—on
a crackajack hoss! She swapped the cuckoo and——"

He broke off to stare at old Cim, who was not
paying a bit of attention to him. For Cimarron
White—foreman of Corral de Terra for the Jessimers in the red past, foreman in this, the red present
—was staring with all the strength of his body and
soul at Jim Grant.

The man from Maine had always reminded Cim
of some one—he'd gone most crazy figuring who.
But now, as Grant was brought to his feet by news
of the peril that faced his daughter, his tall form
looming over them all, his eyes flashing down—Cim
was not wondering—*he knew!* Joyfully, old Cim
knew. And in a voice that stilled every other voice
there, he yelled wildly:

"Lynne Jessimer! Oh—I know you now! *Lynne!*"

All were astounded. Only Kit Kress, the one man
who had always known, could believe the truth.

They saw Cim leap into the buckboard, grasp
Grant's hands and wring them, tears rolling down
his leathery face, which was working with a joy
beautiful and terrible to behold. They heard him
cry:

"Lynne! You ol' son of a gun! You fake dude!
Masquerootin' behind them whiskers! Hidin' out on
your friends!"

"They're goin' to blow up Corral de Terra!"

Swap's voice rose to a shriek. "To-night—they're crossin' the sheep!"

"By mighty, we'll show 'em now!" vengefully roared old Cim. "May Heaven have mercy on their souls—with Lynne to lead!"

Still pressing to see closer, the crowd could not believe Cim. But a pair of chaps were flung at Jim Grant, and he donned them; his gray cap was snatched off, and somebody's sombrero clapped on his head. A brace of six-guns found their way into his hands. And then there was a roar that must have echoed to the sheep camp on the Rio, thunder and all!

"By gravy—it *is* Lynne!"

From mouth to mouth, as fire sweeps through treetops, the cry rang up the street:

"Lynne Jessimer's back!"

All knew him now—all who could be expected to know him. For they saw him now as memory had held him. They saw him with awe. For it was as if he had been resurrected from the grave to lead them. The young men, to whom he was a legend, a hero, martyrized, were crazy as any.

"Take my hoss!" A Los Lobos rider who had fought with Lynne Jessimer in the battle that had been the death of his brothers, and had fought in subsequent battles to avenge those deaths, thrust a bridle into his hands. "It's fast, Lynne!"

And Jim Grant mounted—yet not Jim Grant, but the last Jessimer, Lynne! For with the garb of the range, Lynne put on the ways, the speech, the bitter prejudice of the range. The days at Corral de Terra had been days of trial, fighting for the mastery of self. This day, spent in the old atmosphere, had

been an ordeal, but the self-restraint of thirty years
had held. Now, word that his old home faced de-
struction, the thought of another baptism of blood,
this threat of danger to his daughter, whom he loved
far more than life, swept the thirty intervening years
aside. And he was Lynne Jessimer—dare-devil leader
of the far-famed Lobos!

"Boys"—his black eyes flashed from face to face
—"some of you rode with me once for Corral de
Terra! You heard what he said about my daughter!
Who'll ride with me now?"

Deafening the roar that answered, with nothing
articulate in it but honest, big-souled, savage loyalty
to him. Few had seen Madge, but she was Lynne
Jessimer's daughter, and so, to these old stirrup
brothers of his, the same as blood of their blood,
flesh of their flesh!

Impotent heretofore for lack of a leader, they were
now a mighty force under his leadership. Horses
bunched. Men hastened to mount. All was wild
tumult in the streets of Sundown. Through it, one
grizzled old cowman, drunk with a premature sense
of victory, stood in his stirrups, and swung his sombrero about his head, shouting fiercely:

"Ride, Lobos!"

Wildly the crowd took up the shout. And men,
hearing, rushed in from all sides, thrilled out of
calm reason, rallying blindly, instinctively, hopefully,
to the old battle-cry of the Jessimers.

That cry brought Prosecutor Holt tumbling, coat-
less, hatless, out of his office, to stare after the thun-
dering horses, then pile into the buckboard where
Kit Kress sat like a man turned to stone. For Kit
was seeing Lynne ride away—Kit, who, in the old

days, had been the one man in the country that could ride stirrup to stirrup with Lynne, and who, because of their last memorable ride, was a cripple now and could not go!

But as Holt snatched the reins from him, and applied the lash, and they tore off in the wake of the plunging horses, Kit came to life. *He was following Lynne!* Oh, ignominy to sit in a buckboard when the Lobos rode! But Kit drew cold comfort from the weapon he handled as Holt drove—no innocuous deed or lease, but a black six-gun!

And far behind, on the lone derelict, came Swap Boone, his heart breaking under his old hickory shirt as the storm roared down. Allie was out in this— she was in danger! Nobody cared about *his* baby!

CHAPTER XVIII

WITH the storm coming behind her in a steady, continuous roar, Allie raced down the road that led within five miles of Corral de Terra before branching off at Willow Springs for Devil's Gorge. She was glad, now, *glad* that she wasn't a lady! For no lady could ride as she rode—saddleless, bridleless, with face buried in the pony's neck from the blinding dust that the storm was whipping ahead, bare knees gripping its shoulder pads, wild hair blowing with its mane.

Glad that she wasn't a lady, for no lady could have made that trade! Allie fiercely rejoiced that it was a good trade she had made. She dug her heels into the sorrel's ribs, wildly entreating it to go faster, faster yet, even though she felt it flatten and strain beneath her, and knew it was setting a pace for any horse in that country but Check!

Yet, through it all she remembered that Red Madden had said his gang was waiting for them at Willow Springs, that Mustang's men would be there—waiting for Red Madden and dark, when they were to destroy Corral de Terra. And she realized that they must not see her riding like this—must not see her turn into the road to the gorge! They would stop her from taking warning to Dare, and, warned themselves, would dynamite the ranch before Swap could arouse the cattlemen and go to the aid of the boys out there.

Straining her eyes through the gloom that dust and storm clouds made twilight dark, although it would not be sunset for an hour yet, Allie saw, far ahead, the great, tossing willows that marked the road fork. And, sawing on the rope with all her might, she slowed the pony, turning it off the road to the left, that she might cut over the ridge and, missing the outlaw's rendezvous, come out on the gorge road just above.

Smashing through the moaning sage, and up the slope in reckless and rushing haste, she felt the first large, irregular drops of rain pelting her back. There was a blinding flash, a violent crash, and she dropped her head, stifling her scream on the pony's neck. When, trembling still with the horror of it, she raised her eyes, she was on top of the rise, and saw —down on the gorge road below—five shadowy riders!

Her first mad joy that Red Madden had wasted the time she had spent in hunting Swap and making the trade was killed by a terrible thought—a thing she might have known from the first! With Red Madden ahead, she could not get by! The road followed the canyon all the way—one side of it hugging the steep wall, and the other dropping off into nowhere. There was not a single place where she could circle unseen. If they saw her, they would stop her—and Dare's last chance would be gone! There was no other road!

Half crazed, she looked up at the black mountains, in whose wild heart was the man she loved. Black thoughts crowded her own wild heart, things she had heard of Red Madden—terrible, *true!* He was not human. There was nothing he would not do. All he wanted now was to get his job done—be gone. His job—to kill Dare! Because folks thought Dare was the cattle leader, when he was not a thing of the kind. He had just bought Corral de Terra to give her a chance and because he was a kid, wanting fun! And she saw him laughing up there—like he used to laugh before this black trouble came, saw him "having a picnic" with Madge, saw Red Madden strike like lightning, killing Dare's laugh——

And, completely out of her mind, she started to Dare, where there was not a road! She rode straight over the ridge below which, on the opposite side, Red Madden was traveling, through a wilderness of chasm and cliff, jungling deadfall and boulders, that any sane person would have sworn she could not penetrate.

But the sorrel's blood was up and, goaded by her frantic heels and prayers, he slashed through the brush. Brambles tore Allie's legs, ripped her little, best calico dress into shreds. The storm overtook her, broke over her—such a storm as even the Los Lobos range was stranger to—and her horror of thunderstorms sickened her, so that it took all her strength to cling to her horse, all her courage to keep her eyes open that she might pick out the shortest route to Dare, and keep her bearings by constant glances at that peak that rose above all other peaks— El Capitan.

Over the rough ground she flew, with lightning ripping the sky right open, and thunder rocking the earth. Allie, who was so little, felt so big that the lightning could not possibly miss her. She was sure that every bolt was the one that would kill her, and when it did not and was followed by a startling and pregnant hush, her heart stopped beating in her soul's conviction that the heavens were forging the bolt that would! And she prayed, pitifully: "Don't let it, God! Don't let me get struck—till I get to Dare!"

After that—— She did not think after that. If she beat Red Madden up there and warned Dare, he would save Madge. If she did not save Dare—it didn't matter then what happened to Madge, herself, the old ranch, any of them!

No heights, no depths, had terror for her, only the dread that Red Madden would beat her, and her fear of the storm. And her horse, battling his own fear of it and his rider's, floundered on in mad flight.

Up they stumbled, along a densely timbered ridge that wrestled and moaned in the throttling clutch of the storm. There was a white, blinding, quivering glare, an instantaneous, ear-splitting peal, and Allie screamed in the very ecstasy of fear, as a tree, lightning riven, crashed almost in her path and burst into flame. Wholly unnerved, she thought that Corral de Terra had been blown up, and piteously whimpered:

"You stop 'em, pop!"

Then the rain came in earnest—a terrific downpour, drenching her to the skin, running in streams off the hot coat of the sorrel, making pools they must wallow through, and slopes slick as grease, that they must slide, slip, and slither down at breakneck pace. The black curtain of rain shut out the landscape, hid El Capitan, and Allie was sure she was lost. Frenzied at what would surely happen if she were, she fell to beating the weary and winded sorrel with mad little fists, crying insanely:

"Dare! Dare!"

Tortured by the fancy that she heard him answer, she would jerk her pony in that direction. Then, hearing only the wailing voice of the storm, she would cry again and, imagining him answering from another direction, would turn there, until she was lost in all truth! Lost in the wild and lonely Nimbres, lost with heartbreaking knowledge that Dare was lost, too! Haunted by the memory that she had quarreled with Dare—because she was jealous of him. Oh, she was not jealous now! She had made him think she loved Jasper, that she hated *him!* He must not die—thinking she hated him!

And her fight to find him was as brave and hopeless as her life's struggle against conditions she could not help. She rode up ridges sharper than her agony, down gulfs, deeper, more impassable than the gulf her sensitive heart imagined lay between herself and Madge, along ridges more interminable than all the lonely, dusty roads the *Santa Maria* had traveled. And so she came, at last, to the end of the world, where she looked off into space, and could not go on—for there was no place left to go!

Spent, shaken, chilled, she slipped from her horse and, clinging to him for support, pushed back her sodden hair and looked into space. Dimly she was aware that the storm was over, that the sun had set, and the sky lightened for summer's hour or more of twilight yet. Driftingly, like the ragged clouds racing just over her head, thoughts passed through her mind. Life was like that—the space she looked into. You would be going along, thinking there was no end to it—then you came to the end. And Dare had come to the end of life, thinking——

A tremor shot through her. Joy rested, warmed her. For far down at the end of the space she looked into was—a wagon, horses, tents!

People were coming out of the tents, looking up at the sky. And there—beside the girl in the pretty rose dress that Allie would know anywhere—there was Dare!

The glorious truth burst on her—she had come out on the rim above Devil's Gorge! She had really beaten Red Madden!

CHAPTER XIX

THE WRONG GIRL

CLAMBERING back on her horse, Allie raced out along the jagged rim of that deep precipice, hunting a way to get down. Frantically, as she found none, she sent her voice down: "Dare! Dare!" But it did not reach him. He did not hear. She waved wildly, tried in every way to attract his attention—to let him know that death was riding up that gorge. And, failing, she shrieked again with all the might of her fear, "Dare! Dare!"

He heard! He looked up and around. He saw her now—so high and tiny against the sky, with her arms stretched down. And he waved his sombrero to her, pointed her out to the rest, shouted something to Mace, and ran to Check.

She saw him and Mace saddle and gallop toward her over the level floor of the vast bowl. Then she could not see them for jutting crags, and raced back and forth along the rim, trying to locate them, living an eternity before she heard the ring of iron-shod hoofs, and whirled back to see them scrambling over the brink. Even then she could not get to them, for a deep fissure lay between. And, as they started around, she motioned them back, crying hysterically:

"Dare, Red Madden's blowin' up Corral de Terra —at dark!"

"*What!*" They both jerked up.

"They're dynamitin' the old ranch—to get the cowmen away from the ford—while they cross the sheep——"

Mace wheeled. But Dare held back, staring at her. His face was anxious, and his worried, "Are you all right, Allie?" eased the pain that had been in her heart for weeks.

"Yes, yes, Dare! But Red Madden's——"

He had turned, and to her dismay, both men started back down the trail they had come—to take the gorge road to the ranch. They would meet Red Madden coming up!

"No!" she screamed. *"This* way—it's shortest, Dare!"

"Can I make it?" he flashed, swinging back.

"I made it!" Pride sang through that cry.

Then they were gone and, faint from the reaction, Allie slumped down on her horse, only to spring up at a fearful thought and lash madly after him, crying insanely, *"Dare!"*

But he was out of all hearing. And she pulled up, nerveless, stunned, bitterly sobbing. *Madge!* What had she done! Dare would never forgive her for sending away the only men who could protect Madge. He might think she did it on purpose— *wanted* Madge stolen! And there was not a man down there but Biggers and Jasper—oh, what could she do!

In her extremity, a plan came to Allie—a wild, weird plan, and a kind of rapture that buoyed her courage. If she could do *that,* Dare would have to forgive her. He could never forget her!

Galloping around the ravine to take the trail down to camp, Allie saw, far, far down the mountainside, the thread of a road that serpentined into the gorge. And on it—mere dots in the distance—were five, toiling riders, leading an extra horse. Red Madden! She had hardly ten minutes at best!

She kicked her pony down the trail Dare had come up, a trail hazardous at any pace, all but suicidal taken like this—headlong, with eyes closed to the dizzying drop, slipping, sliding, stumbling, falling— but she won the level at last. Urging the sorrel to a last desperate burst of speed, she raced toward the campers who stood shocked with the horror of watching her mad descent, shocked now by sight of her white, scared face, and by the terrible news she flung at them:

"Red Madden's comin'!" she loudly shouted.

Warning them that the fate of Corral de Terra, of the whole Los Lobos range, might depend on their keeping still and letting her do the talking, she slid to the ground and, seizing Madge Grant, dragged her into the nearest tent.

"Quick," she panted, "take off your clothes!" Realizing herself the necessity for rapid action, she was appalled to see—as she yanked her own wet little shred of a dress over her head and flung it at Madge —that the stunned girl had not begun to disrobe.

"Take off your clothes!"

"Are you crazy?" Madge cried, with every reason to believe from Allie's actions and looks that she was. "I certainly will not!"

Allie stepped toward her, her eyes unnaturally big and awesomely black and bright. "You will!" she threatened. "Or I'll strip you!"

One second the girls stared at each other—the ragamuffin and the lovely patrician, savage and sophisticate, Allie and Madge! Madge's eyes fell; her hand went tremblingly to her sash.

"I got a good reason"—Allie's lips quivered—"or I wouldn't ask you to do it, Madge!"

Completely under the spell of her, Madge obeyed, with a haste she was never able to understand. One by one, as she removed her outer garments, Allie put them on. She was tying the trim shoe, when she looked up, saw Madge still in her underslip, and commanded:

"Put my dress on!"

Madge lifted it with willing spirit, but her flesh shrank from it—soiled, cold, dripping wet. Allie saw her shrink, and shame swept her soul.

"It won't kill you!" she cried bitterly. "You can stand it—once!"

And as Madge put it on, her beauty dimmed like a turned-down lamp. It was extinguished utterly, when Allie snatched up the pail of water that stood in the tent, and threw the contents over her golden head!

"Allie," sputtered the girl, wrenching away, "why are you doing this? What's going to happen?"

"Nothing—to you," Allie said wearily, the sound of hoofs striking hard on her heart. "Nothing to any one that matters—much. Not if you keep still —let me do the talkin'!"

But Madge was not listening. She was staring at Allie, seeing—what she had always wanted to see— Allie Boone properly dressed, in the very dress she had schemed to give her, and the result was even lovelier than she had dreamed! Why, that rose crape sports frock *belonged* to Allie! Oh, she was glad she had brought it; though it was too elaborate for a mountain camp. She had worn it because she loved fragile and feminine things——

"Wait, Allie"—Madge was far too absorbed to hear Red Madden's men reining in by the tent—"the skirt's too long!" Deftly she bloused it a bit over the sash, gave her a pull here, and a pat there. "You're so white, Allie! You need just a touch of rouge—it will make your eyes twice as bright!" Expertly, while Allie pressed her hands to her heart to still its tumult, Madge put back in her cheeks the color the ride, and the coming ordeal, had robbed her of. Then, brushing Allie's wet, black curls into some kind of order, she jammed on them a little white-felt hat, and, holding her off, looking at her with some of the creator's pride of achievement, she cried: "Oh, Allie, you're stunning!"

Allie's eyes filled with longing and tears. She whispered a last wish—for she did not doubt that Red Madden would kill her when he found out that she was not Madge:

"Please tell Dare how I looked."

"But, Allie, we'll show him when he——"

"Where's Devlyn?" From just outside the tent a voice—that harsh, ugly voice she remembered—demanded. And Allie trembled now, as when she had heard it, through the *Santa Maria's* canvas walls.

Nobody answered, and she thought mirthlessly that Dare's dudes were not finding it half so much fun to meet Red Madden as they had imagined. But, no—they were waiting for her to do the talking!

"Remember," tensely, she whispered to Madge, "No matter what comes up—you be still!"

Then, parting the tent flaps, she stepped leisurely out.

There, grouped just as she had left them, Mrs.
Mills, Jasper, Eloise, Biggers, and the rest were
staring at the horsemen in the fascination of fear.
There was Red Madden—the big, burly, cold-eyed
brute that his voice had painted for her—and his
four picked men—all of the same villainous aspect.
Birds of a feather flocked together for just such
deeds as this!

Allie saw Corral de Terra's guests start as they
saw her. She saw in their eyes—especially Jasper's
—that she was as pretty as she had dreamed of being.
But she did not know that it was not merely because
the exquisite clothes for the first time revealed her
beauty, but for a glory in her face—the glory of
a woman who flinches at no sacrifices. She knew
one instant of torturing suspense lest they betray her,
then horror, as Madden's cold eyes, turning on her,
flamed with hot greed, and a look that said plainly:
"This is the girl!"

"Where's Devlyn?" he snapped.

A trembling seized her, a dizzy faintness that she
fought with all the strength of her being. She had
played "lady" all her life for fun. She must
play it now for the sake of the girl Dare loved!
And drawing herself up to her full five-feet-one, she
looked Red Madden up and down with a cold ap-
praisal that made him squirm.

"Who wants to know?" was her cool request.

Mentally cursing her for a rich man's brat, he thundered in a tone meant to make her squirm, grovel
to him: *"Red Madden!"*

She yawned! So Mrs. Mills and the rest all declared, when they could bring themselves to speak
calmly of little Allie again. But Allie knew it was

terror that she choked back—successfully, for there
was none in her careless remark:

"Whoever *he* is." She shrugged disdain. "But
his whereabouts is no secret. This girl"—supercili-
ously pointing to the drenched and bedraggled, little
waif that was Madge—"just rode into camp with
news that there was trouble at the ranch, and Mr.
Devlyn took French leave of us."

She had exploded a bomb in the enemies' ranks.
The quintet cursed, and exchanged startled glances.
But their leader's eyes now evilly narrowed on her.

"We didn't meet Devlyn! How do you account
for that?"

"I don't." Allie's black eyes looked straight up
into his with a scorn that made him squirm again.
"But I dare say," she coldly added, "it was because
he went over the mountains. A short cut, he said.
It's the way this girl came."

"Red," swiftly intruded one of the gang, "that's
straight! This kid, here"—contemptuously he indicated Madge Grant—"looks like a drowned rat! She's
sure been out in the storm. An' take a look at her
hoss, there! Boss, there's been a slip-up! The cowmen's wise! What'll we do?"

Swinging his horse about, Red Madden snapped:
"Grab the girl—an' burn the breeze back!"

Before the horrified group could comprehend, two
men leaped down and sprang at Allie. One of them
held her, while the other slipped a rope over her
head. She went wild at their touch, fought them
with teeth and nails, like a little tigress, gave them
a tussle, forgot in her terror that this was what she
wanted, that it meant the success of her plan. But
she did not forget she was acting the lady, though

she forgot to act like the real ladies she had met and rage helplessly after the fashion of Lady Charlotte, her old heroine: "How dare you! How dare you! Unhand me, villains!"

And Jasper Kade, roused to a better self by this outrage to the girl he loved—for contrary to Dare's belief, Jasper loved Allie Boone—sprang to her aid, only to be ruthlessly felled, insensible, by a gun butt in one vigilant outlaw's hand. Another fanned his weapon on Biggers, who was only a jump behind.

"Stick 'em up, my festive gent," he ordered Ezra, "or you'll go down—an' stay down!"

In a twinkling, Allie was bound, and tied on the back of the extra horse. Red Madden took the lead rope. "Tell Jim Grant," he instructed, quirting her horse and putting spurs to his own, "that he'll hear from us later!"

And Madge, white as snow, in sudden divination of what was happening, seeing in a flash how cleverly, how nobly, Allie was sacrificing herself, and knowing her reason for doing it, ran after them, pleading:

"Wait! You've got the wrong girl! I'm Madge Grant!"

Game to the last, Allie twisted around in her bonds, crying scornfully: "Why, you—you *wagon tramp!*"

But Red Madden, storming away with his captive, would not fall for a crude play like that. You couldn't fool him! This girl was the real thing! He knew a lady, when he saw one!

CHAPTER XX

RIDE, Lobos!" After thirty years, that cry was lifted in the Los Lobos Range, electrifying as the storm that militant band of cowmen rode through, terrifying to those who had cause to fear it as to Allie had been the storm. And the echoes caught it up, the thunder bore it along—*"Ride, Lobos!"*

And they rode—grizzled old Lobos, who had ridden to it in their mad youth; eager lads, who, like Dare Devlyn, had regretted that they had been born too late to hear it, now thrilled to it, and rode. Out of Sundown, out over the range, they swept with the storm, their numbers swelling mysteriously, as though the wild cry summoned phantom riders out of their graves to ride!

On, in a dark and plunging mass, now hidden by the black curtain of rain, now revealed by a white and dazzling flash, now shaking the ground with the beat of their hoofs, now silent, as thunder killed all sound of them in the beat of its own, infernal tattoo. Yet on and on—— Where? *Where Lyne Jessimer led!* They would have followed had they known that Death rode with every man of them this night!

Fanatical, their faith in Lynne Jessimer; boundless, their love for him. With awe in their eyes, they watched him, riding ahead of them with a grace and daring that mocked the thirty years that had intervened. If his return was a matter of awe, greater their awe that he had returned the same, still could ride with the reckless skill that made him now, as in the old days, the best rider ever known on that range!

The nearest man was twenty paces behind, when Lynne swerved off the road and swept in the gate of the Seven Up Ranch, dashed up to the house, and under the window of this loyal cowman stirringly cried:

"Lobos, ride!"

And the old rancher within all but overturned the supper table as he sprang up, staring eyed at hearing that command in a dead man's voice! He ran outside, to see the shadowy forms riding off through the rain, made sure of the state of his gun even as he ran to his horse, with no thought on earth but to obey that command!

On again, leaving the road, to cut over to the Hondoo Ranch, stunning the men who were nervously fiddling away time in the bunk house out of the storm, that cry that rang in their ears like the trumpet of the Angel Gabriel: "Lobos, ride!"

So on, from ranch to ranch. Men went to fight, and women were left behind to weep. Fast as they rode, the storm went faster, and blew over. Then the sky grew light. The sage glistened, filling the air with its sweetness as it was macerated under the pounding hoofs. At one place or another the whole Los Lobos range was in the saddle to-night!

And still this company storming over the plains had only a vague idea of their threefold purpose— to rescue Madge Jessimer—as she must be called now—from Cull Cole's hirelings, avert the disaster

to Corral de Terra, and prevent the sheep crossing
the Rio ford. But in what order, or by what tactics,
they did not know. And still their leader gave no
sign.

What was Lynne Jessimer thinking? What does
any father think whose daughter is in deadly danger?
Not—Heaven forbid!—the thoughts Lynne had as
he rode. For he thought that destiny had drawn him
a continent across, back to the scene of his crimes
—for such, in his steady and blameless life as Jim
Grant, he had seen them to be—that the daughter he
loved might be delivered over into the enemies' hands,
and a fitting punishment meted out to him! And
the thought of his old sins being visited on her
aroused a shuddering cataclysm within him. And
but for Madge, Jim Grant might have never existed,
for his was the spirit of the wild youth he had
been! But, as he rode, faster than his fastest fol-
lower, the faces of dead men rode with him, men
dead because he had once constituted himself an
avenger of blood! And they haunted and taunted
him—had a ghastly, ghostly, last laugh on him!

And yet, through all his anguish surged a strange
exultation that with him were riding at least twenty
of his old fighting band—men who would die for
him, whose repute for fearlessness was known
throughout the whole Southwest. With them, he
was invincible, nor could destiny, Red Madden, all
the sheep cohorts, or the very powers of darkness,
prevail against him!

To get them, Lynne had dared this delay. If Red
Madden surprised the camp, killed Dare, and made
off with Madge, Lynne would need men he could
bank on. If Allie Boone got there in time to warn

the picnickers, he could depend on Dare and Mace standing the gang off until help came. With his daughter safe, he would pay his debt to these men, repay faith with faith, help them settle, in one grand sweep, their problem of the range.

Such were his thoughts, as he swept over the prairie swell and came in sight of Willow Springs. Here, the roads forked, and his eyes, burning on the willows, saw them alive with horses and men. He did not know Red Madden's plans—only what Swap had told him. He did not know that these were Mustang's men, waiting for their leader. But, almost in the same instant, he saw pandemonium spring among them, as one shouted excitedly, pointing up to the ridge above. His own eyes darted up to see the cause of their consternation and, in the cold fear that seized him, he forgot all about them, pulling his foaming horse up.

Far down over the brown of that ridge—where the sight of Red Madden on the road below had driven Allie into the hills—streaked a vividly checked, black-and-white horse. Just as it dropped into a draw, a second rider slashed into veiw, frantically spurring his slower mount.

"By hickory," yelled old Cim, plunging up with the rest of the band, "that's Dare an' Mace! What are they doin' here? What does it mean?

It meant but one thing to Lynne—that Red Madden had taken Madge and the boys were coming for help! And, as the flying paint rose over the last low ridge and swooped down toward them, the distracted father spurred savagely to meet him, followed by his loyal clan.

Sliding Check to a stop, Dare suppressed the

astonishment that rose to his lips at sight of Jim
Grant, the rich promoter from Maine. *Could* this be
Grant? This tight-mouthed, burning-eyed, grim-
looking man in chaps and sombrero and sagging
guns! This skilled rider pulling in a foam-lashed,
spirited horse with the iron hand of a born range
man!

"Where's Madge?"

Dare started at Grant's voice, sharp with suspense.
"Why," he said blankly, "up to camp with the
rest."

"Has Red Madden been there?"

Dare could only look his amazement. "Nobody's
been there—but Allie," he told them, wondering who
these men were, why Cim was here if there was
trouble at Corral de Terra. "That game li'le kid
rode up through the storm to tell us Madden was
goin' to blow up the ranch!"

"She didn't tell you"—Grant's eyes seemed burning a hole right through him—"that the outlaws were
going to kidnap Madge?"

"No!" Dare cried, whitening. "Can you ask
that? Would I be here?"

"Of course not! Forgive me, son! I'm——"

"Look, Lynne!" roared Cim, throwing an arm toward the willows. "Those men—there's something
crooked down there! They went plumb loco when
they spotted us here! I'll gamble they're Red Madden's gang!"

As, tensely, all watched, the men swept out of the
trees and across the dry bed of the stream.

"They're lightin' out for Corral de Terra!" cried
Jessimer. "Boy"—he swung on Dare, who was
stunned by that "Lynne!"—"take half these men

an' go on! . Protect your property. If they get inside those adobe walls, they can stand the whole country off! I'm goin' to Madge!"

"So am I!" the boy flamed. For the truth he had glimpsed fleetingly had now flashed on him, raising every drop of hot blood in his veins, setting his heart hammering with the thought of riding with the last Jessimer. "Besides Madge—I'm responsible for them folks up there! Send Mace, here—an' Cim!"

Watching the man he had known as Jim Grant quickly divide the cowmen by riding his horse through the band, Dare could not understand how he had been so blind. No wonder Grant had range savvy! No wonder he knew Western horses! No wonder he looked like Kit, Cim, all the Los Lobos old-timers! No wonder he had gone to pieces that first day in the court and prayed for strength! Lynne Jessimer! Then Madge——

"Boys," Jessimer said to half of that band, "go with Cim. Hold Corral de Terra till we come!"

Instantly, with Cim in the lead, they plunged off after the outlaws galloping down the main road. And Jessimer, Dare, and the rest of the men, spurred across the brushy wastes for the gorge. Suddenly, as they came from behind some screening foliage, they were dismayed to see that the gang had divided. Part of them were swerving to the left and racing for the mouth of the canyon.

"They've split!" cried Lynne. "The main band's gone to the ranch, but the rest is tryin' to head us off! That means Madden's up the gorge! Boys, if they beat us to that pass we'll never get by!" And he settled down to ride, as he had not ridden yet.

But there was one who could ride with Lynne now, stirrup to stirrup, ride just as recklessly—a lad after his own wild heart. Dare even held the paint pony in to ride with Lynne in that mad race for the pass. If Madden's men beat them to the narrow neck of the canyon in which ran the road to Devil's Gorge, they could fortify themselves in the rocks and stand Lynne's men off until Madge was carried to some safe hiding place! The rescuers' one hope lay in reaching the pass first. And the outlaws had a road beneath them, and the advantage of a long start!

"There ain't a horse livin' can make it!" Lynne groaned.

But Dare shouted: "Check can—or come mighty near it!"

"Then go to it, boy! Hold 'em back—we'll be right behind!"

Proud to play such a part, proud to show off his horse, Dare crouched lower, gave Check his head, touched him with the spurs, and thrilled to the paint's instant response. Out ahead of the rest he ran, smooth, clean, fleet as the flight of an eagle. They had left the cowmen far behind, when Dare's exultance at the victory he saw in sight changed to despair, as his eyes, riveted on the running outlaws, saw a long chestnut shoot out ahead of the rest, in the low, flowing stride of a trained race horse. And it had a beaten track. A hundred-yard start!

Dare lost hope there. Nevertheless, he said in Check's ear, man to man: "Boy, give me all you got! I never asked you before! The game's stacked on you, Check—but do the best you can!"

The wind roared in his ears, and the landscape went skimming in Check's loyal answer to that appeal.

Above the wind of his running came shots! And oddly Dare thought of that other ride to the tune of them—that night when he had stubbornly sown the seeds of the grim harvest this night was reaping. That ride had seemed real, when he had every reason to believe it a sham. This one *was real,* but he could not believe it was not faked. He could hardly believe that men were actually shooting at him, though bullets came convincingly close! Then, wrenching his gaze from the straining chestnut on that diminishing strip of road, he saw the running outlaws level at him, saw the smoke of their guns, heard, closer, the sinister, leaden whine, and there surged up in him that intense anger which comes to most men under fire for the first time, a crazy passion to kill—kill——

Now, skimming over a sage flat that gave out on the road just before it entered the canyon, he heard a popping behind him, and knew that Lynne's men were attracting the fire away from him. He saw an outlaw throw up his hands and pitch to the ground, and an empty saddle hurtle along. Then the fringing brush of the canyon came between, hiding his view. Lucky—for it spoiled theirs, too, and they could not see to shoot at him! And now, though he knew Check could never beat the racer, Dare spurred the harder, formulating a daring scheme in his mind.

He could cut in behind the chestnut, crowd him so close that his rider would have no chance to dismount and take ambush, cut off the rest of the outlaws, and hold them back until the cowmen came! A big order! A fatal order—had he known what he knew five minutes later. But it is doubtful if he would have hesitated, for his heart was on fire and caution was forgotten.

Intent on getting the maximum of speed out of Check, Dare swerved into the road, a hundred yards ahead of the outlaws and hard on the heels of the chestnut. Behind him, the fire kept up unremittingly. But it was between the outlaws and the cattlemen, for no bullets sang. Then the rider ahead—Mustang, though Dare did not know it—dashed into the mouth of the gorge. The boy drew his gun, expecting him to whirl, dismount, and, from cover of the rocks, defend the road. Dare was astonished to see him pound straight on! His breath caught at the thought that the fellow was going to warn the men who had gone for Madge, and he knew a frightful second of indecision. Check might overtake that rider in a long chase, but then the outlaws would cut off the cattlemen. His job was to hold the road for Lynne!

Sliding Check in behind a great boulder that commanded the entrance, Dare jumped down, his face set hard as the rocks his gun hand rested upon. And when the first outlaw appeared, instantly, cool as ever Lynne Jessimer did, the boy drew bead on his living target and fired!

The fellow's horse reared, making half circles with his hind legs, blocking those behind him. A dozen guns opened on him. Bullets smashed against the rock. And Dare, wholly in the grip of the battle frenzy, shot and shot. He was amazed to see that his shots had no other effect than to throw them in a panic and hold them off. What was the matter with him? Suddenly, he knew what was wrong! But he kept on, pouring smoke into their faces, until the outlaws, demoralized at being hemmed in between two fires, turned a deadly volley at the oncoming cowmen and dashed off into the brush, utterly routed.

Dare emerged from behind the rock as the cattlemen came to a stop.

"Great work!" one applauded.

"For a bluff!" the boy made sheepish apology, looking up into the face of Lynne, and seeing it queerly strained and gray again. "My gun was loaded with blanks! I plumb forgot to change 'em after——" He broke off in swift alarm, springing forward, as Lynne Jessimer swayed in the saddle, and caught him as he fell.

"Good grief!" quaveringly cried an old Lobo. "They got Lynne!"

Numbed by this disaster, the men flung themselves down and carried their old comrade to the roadside, eased him gently to the wet grass, and would have looked to his wound, but he stayed them in an agony that came from no physical hurt.

"It's nothing!" he gasped, with a courage that brought tears to the rugged cheeks bending over. "Leave me, boys—go to *her!*"

His failing sight singled out Dare. "Boy"—Dare felt his imploring gaze, though his eyes were too him to see—"you've heard of the Lobos. You're ridin' with them! God never made braver men. Take them—an' bring me my daughter!"

Silently, Dare pressed his hand and, stooping, unbuckled Lynne's cartridge belt and guns. In the trouble coming he would not be armed with blanks! Then, commanding one of the cowmen to stay with

Lynne, he turned about to see every eye fixed on him.

An old leader had fallen before the night's work was begun. Another of the same stamp had been raised—the youth whom they had expected to take the lead when the crisis came, the youth who, because of his connection with Corral de Terra, and because they sensed the same dare-devil quality in him, stood in their eyes for the Jessimers.

So fate forced Dare Devlyn, at last, to the head of the cattle faction. And he was glad. Circumstances placed him at the head of the Lobos, and he was proud of it! He was a fit leader, with his young face aame with battle-fire and heat. Even the silver trappings on Check, his own rich and picturesque dress, set him apart, and gave these grim followers pride and confidence in him, as did the wit and nerve he had already shown.

Long ago seemed the night when Dare had sat in the river camp thrilling to Swap's story of Lynne Jessimer. Now he was setting forth on what might have been the same red trail—to avenge the Jessimers!

Snatching his bridle, he leaped on Check and spun him about. Strangely, there sprang to his lips the Jessimers' old range cry, "Lobos, ride!" And madly, then, up the wild gorge, they followed their new leader—a wild, reckless youth, on a fast, flashy paint!

CHAPTER XXI

GRAY as the lowering skies, gray as the gloom in the grim, gray canyon of rocks, were Dare's thoughts as he rode at the head of the Lobos. He thought of Madge, even now in the hands of those ruffians, of what might have happened to his guests —folks who had trusted their safety to him—of what would occur at the ford on the Rio, and of what would take place at Corral de Terra, if Cim did not beat the outlaws there!

Torturingly, his brain pictured Las Vegas, Sam, and the boys, lazing at the ranch, as ignorant of trouble as he had been an hour ago; the outlaws storming the court, overwhelming them, killing them! Then the coming of the Lobos with Cim! He saw, in blank imagination, old Cim, who had pleaded with him not to risk rousing the passions he foolishly had unleashed, going down in the fight—because he, Dare, had not listened! He saw the grass-trampled, flower-crushed court sprinkled with a scarlet rain that was not the petals of shepherd's clock—but blood! More blood on the old house! More blood on his hands!

Hauntingly, Dare thought of Allie, wondered why she had not told him about Madge. And his hot heart cried: "But it ain't no wonder if she got muddled! The wonder is that that brave li'le girl made it at all!"

Yes, he had wondered that every step of the way coming down over the selfsame ground! And she had *climbed* it in the dark of the storm. He could not bear to think of it—of what might have happened to her. And he could see her yet—her white, pinched face, all eyes, staring at him across that wash; he could hear her bravely crying to him: *"I made it, Dare!"*

"She loved the ol' ranch so much," was his ready excuse, "that in danger to it, she forgot about Madge!"

Oh, these, and a thousand more thoughts of the same black ilk came to Dare in his ride. Yet through all his fire of conjecture, and plan, and torturing surmise, he was alert every instant, scanning the gray rocks in the gray gloom, lest he run into a trap. He had no hope of reaching the camp before Madden. He knew the renegade would be warned by the rider on the fast horse. This rider might even have met Madden bringing Madge out, and the gang would be lying in wait for them around some of these bends. He realized that if he was to rescue Madge and restore her to her father in the little time Lynne might have on earth, he must cool down. He realized, too, that he was outriding the Lobos, and reined in Check, for in a fight he would be helpless without them.

Riding in the comparative quiet then, he heard hoofs thudding around the next bend!

Quickly, he pulled to the roadside. His hand dropped to his gun. But his heart gave a mighty bound as the horse galloped around the turn—a buckskin, spent, sweat-drenched, one of the team that had hauled the wagon to camp! And on him, a small, bare-legged figure in a red dress!

His glad cry, "Allie!" died on his lips, for Allie did not ride like that—all over her horse! And about the white oval of her face beat no curls of dusk, but a halo of gold! Not Allie—*Madge!*

Yet, as he leaped down and lifted her from her horse, a cold terror seized him, grew on him each moment she clung to him, crying hysterically, unable to tell him a word. The Lobos pounded up, ringed about, staring at them, cheering—as one of them told the rest who she was. Those cheers turned into fierce imprecations, as she cried to Dare, pity in her wet eyes for him:

"Red Madden's got Allie!" Madge felt the tremor that went through him. "She saved me, Dare! She made me change clothes with her! I didn't realize what she was doing. I couldn't have let her sacrifice herself for me—she's worth any number of me! But she—I was afraid of her, Dare! And she carried it through, made Red Madden believe she was me. Oh, she was wonderful! I can't tell you."

She did not need to! Had not he seen Allie acting in a faded Navajo blanket in the wrecked old house? Couldn't he see her now, dressed like Madge, up in that wild setting, fooling a fiend whose name was a dread through the Southwest!

"They struck down Jasper when he tried to save her!" Madge cried, seeing Dare change before her eyes—age, harden—knowing that he, who had been blind had received his sight; "He came to—wild! He *loves* her, Dare! He and I followed——"

"Which way did they go?" The sudden intensity of that startled her.

"They started this way. But they met some one just above here—we could see by the tracks—and cut off toward El Capitan! Jasper followed them. I came on. Oh, they'll kill her, Dare, when they find out!"

Hoarse anger ran through the ranks of the Lobos.

Gently, Dare took hold of Madge, sorry for her, even in this moment of stark revelation. "Madge, you'll find your father down the canyon. Go on— he needs you. Yes"—in answer to the terrified question she looked—"he's hurt!"

Then Dare and the Lobos were gone!

And the girl went on—a million miles it seemed in her grief, with a million turnings in every one. For, at every one, she expected, feared, prayed to see her father, who was down here—hurt! Oh, these things didn't happen except in books! They weren't *let* happen! It wasn't real!

At length, she came to the mouth of the canyon. A buckboard stood in the road. Three men were lifting a limp figure in. She cried out to them, slid down, and ran toward her father. But they thought she was Allie, and tried to keep her away from him. And she had to explain Red Madden's mistake all over again.

"Lass," Kit Kress said gently, helping her in, "nothin's ever as bad as it seems. A bullet more ain't goin' to kill Lynne. I fixed him up as best I could till we git him home."

She seemed not to notice that they called him "Lynne." And crouched down in the back of the wagon, she held her father's head in her lap, telling him she was safe, knowing he did not hear, nor feel the tears on his still face.

So, with Kit driving, Holt beside him, and the cowman Dare had left with Lynne coming behind with the buckskin, they started off at a funeral pace. Kit could not see much of the road for thinking *how* he was riding with Lynne—that Lynne was riding in a buckboard!

"Better take him home—or to town?" he asked, as they came to the forks of the road.

"Home," said Prosecutor Holt.

"There's trouble there."

"There'll be trouble everywhere!"

Just as they turned into the main road, two riders came up behind them, throwing mud in their faces as they galloped past.

"Sheepmen!" snapped Kit, recognizing Joe Philips. "Cull Cole's side-kick! On their way to help wreck Corral de Terra!"

"Hardy, dang him!" swore Holt, recognizing the other rider as the ex-sheriff. "He must feel almighty proud of himself to-night! A good man gone wrong! If he'd ever served that warrant on Cole——"

His face hardened. Kit passed the reins to his left hand, ominously freeing his right. For the men, recognizing them, had whirled and were coming back.

"Holt," Hardy cried in great agitation, pulling up at that side of the rig, "what's this I hear about blowin' up Corral de Terra an' abductin' a girl?"

"Truth!" scathingly lashed out the county attorney. "The truth you might have expected to hear when you put your personal interests ahead of the range at large! The sort of truth that shocks decent men when a sheriff lies down on the job—and there is no law, when hired fighters are brought in and take the situation out of the hands of responsible men; when a mob rules by violence, and nobody's interests, nobody's property, no man, woman, or child is safe!"

"Is it true that Lobos are ridin'?" cried Philips, as Hardy sat speechless from the attack. "They say Lynne Jessimer's leadin' 'em!"

"The Lobos are ridin'," was the stormy response, "but Dare Devlyn's heading them!"

"*Did* Lynne come back!" pressed Philips tensely.

Kit Kress turned on him an anguished face that quivered in wrath. "Take a look in the back of the buckboard an' see! *That's* Lynne! Take a good, long look at him! He rallied the Lobos to save his daughter from that rapscallion, an' that's what your hired guns done to him!"

Awed, the men looked at the broken figure, at the weeping girl.

"*She's* safe, then." Hardy was husky with relief.

"She's safe," Holt said coldly, "because Red Madden made a mistake. He's got Swap Boone's little girl, instead! Men, I leave it to you to figure what he'll do, when he finds out her father's just a tramp trader—not worth two cents!"

A terrible silence followed, while they thought.

"Holt," Hardy cried earnestly, "*we* ain't to blame!"

"Your hired guns——"

"Holt"—Hardy raised his right hand—"I swear the sheepmen did not know of this! Oh, there's a renegade or two among us—same as there is among you, but the bulk of us wouldn't have stood for this! I'm a sheepman—an' I'm a *man!* So's Joe, here! He rebelled before ever these things come up! An' when it comes to abductin' girls—— Holt, what can we do?"

"What can we do?" echoed the prosecuting attorney, stimulated to a wan hope by his tone. "What can we do?" His pocketed hand closed over something hard and smooth. "Our duty, Hardy—or die in the attempt! I doubt if it can be checked now. There's one way it might——"

He drew his hand from his pocket, and extended it to ex-Sheriff Hardy. Dully, a sheriff's star gleamed in his palm, the star Hardy had relinquished to protect his interests, the star that had been offered to many, and by as many refused. A brave man, he who would accept it this night.

A brave man—Sheriff Hardy was pinning it on!

CHAPTER XXII

THE WHITE FLAG

"HEAVEN pity us one, an' pity us all, if ever Los Lobos wakes up!" had been the cry of Kit Kress that long-ago day when Dare had complained of its being a sleepy old range. Heaven pity Dare now, racing ahead of the Lobos, charging his soul with its awakening! Blind fool that he had been— in more ways than one! He saw now what Madge had meant when she said he was blind. He had looked deep into his heart of hearts, and saw no divinity there, but a regular little human, a little gypsy, with lupines in her hair—cute as a kitten's ear! And he knew in every beat of his anguished heart that he loved Allie Boone—not with any humble devotion, but as a man loves a woman! He had been furious at the thought of Madge at Red Madden's mercy, but Allie——

He moaned: "I'll go loco thinkin'!"

Spurring Check as ruthlessly as cruel anxiety spurred himself, Dare crashed up the canyon. If ever they were to rescue Allie, it must be in the next half hour, before night closed down, hiding the tracks. He came to the place where the outlaws had met the lone rider and turned off the road. Their horses had dug deep furrows in the soft earth where they slid down the bank to the canyon floor, plainly marking the spot.

With no slackening of pace, Dare spurred Check over, made in safety the perilous slide, dashed over the gravelly bed of the dry stream at the bottom, and picked up the outlaws' tracks on the opposite bank with hardly a second's loss of time. Tearing up the slope, he glanced back, and saw the Lobos as recklessly making the plunge.

"Thank God for Allie's sake," he cried in warm gratitude, "that the Lobos are ridin' again!"

Swiftly, with only his convulsive breathing to tell of the strain, Check gained the first ridge, and galloping now on a comparatively level trail around a horn of the mountain all but ran down a man, rolling about on his saddleless mount. It was Jasper— on the other buckskin! But for his horse, Dare would never have known him. For Jasper looked nothing like the bored and anæmic young cub he had met at the depot! His plastered hair straggled down over his face, which was all stained from that ugly cut on his forehead, and his hawkish eyes were as bloodthirsty as those of a savage!

"Thank Heaven, Devlyn!" he cried in joy and surprise, as Check tore up. "You've come in time! Those scoundrels just dropped over that rim! They're heading for the ranch. She's tied to her horse— *hurry*, Devlyn!"

Dare needed no urging. As he pounded on, up the base of El Capitan, thoughts smote his quivering heart, pang on pang. Jasper loved Allie! He had been in earnest all the time! *He* hadn't been blind! He had been all over the world and knew there wasn't another girl like Allie in it! And he, Dare, had told Allie that Jasper was making a fool of her! And she, loving Jasper, knew that Dare himself had been the fool! No wonder she hated him!

And, as Check heroically struggled and strained on a rock-strewn pitch, Dare thought of what might have been. No bitterer thoughts are known to man! He remembered Allie's kiss that morning of parting, the touch of her lips, the soft clasp of her arms. Oh, he had known even then! He remembered her on the fateful eve of her return—stepping out of the shadows to meet him, his name on her lips, joy in her eyes. And he—she might have loved him then—if he hadn't been blind! He had been jealous of Jasper then, jealous, in his blindness, ever since! And now Red Madden had Allie—tied to her horse and——

Here Check pulled over the rim, and Dare's eyes winged down to Corral de Terra, in the deeper gloom of El Capitan. Vaguely, in that flashing glance, he noted dark figures running about the court, two bands of riders, against the lighted gray of the wall—the outlaws and Cim's Lobos, almost in a dead heat in their race for the ranch! But which was first, he could not have told had he tried to. But he did not try, for streaming out, at the foot of the mountain, were the men he sought!

With unerring instinct, he picked out Madden on the giant black, leading another horse, on which was a brighter, lighter, *littler* rider—Allie, in Madge's dress! And black fury possessed Dare at thought of the terrific racking her slight body was standing. What if her horse fell, rolled on her, crushed her—tied that a way. Wild, as he rode came the cry of the Lobos behind him—sighting their quarry!

Down treacherous shale, through chaparral, down

toward the river, Dare raced, his eyes never leaving Allie or her captor. He was glad that he had spent a thousand dollars for a horse when he made his splurge, wishing to Heaven he'd spent it all—so he couldn't have bought the old ranch and thus delivered Allie into Red Madden's hands! Why was he taking her to Corral de Terra? Dare saw but one reason. Madden did not know that the whole country was raised against him. He planned to give the men in the canyon the slip, cut over to his gang who would have taken the ranch, reorganize, finish his dastardly work for the sheepmen, and slip away at dark with his captive.

Shots! They were fighting at Corral de Terra. And Madden was dragging Allie there!

Below him the outlaws plunged through the creek, and swung south to circle the ranch and join their men on the other side where the fight was in progress. And Dare, wild at the thought of Allie in that deadly hail, cut straight down toward the gate in the river wall. He must warn the boys to look out for Allie! Then, reënforced by his Lobos, they would overwhelm the gang with their full strength.

Galloping, now, in a bee line, he saw that the Lobos had turned with him. He was nearing the cottonwoods of Swap's camp, when there was a terrible blast, the sickening feeling of quaking earth, and an onrush of horror that weakened him. The outlaws had taken Corral de Terra—blown it up! And that meant—— Las Vegas, Sam—— More empty saddles!

As Dare dashed up the trail, with no break in Check's furious pace, the whole scene—walls, buildings, court—was obscured by a mighty, enveloping cloud of dust. Through a shower of débris falling out of the cloud, he tore up to the gate in the river wall.

Here men blocked his path. A gun was leveled on him. And, above the bedlam in the court, a young maniac with Sam's voice shouted:

"Don't, Mace! It's Check!"

As Mace, unnerved by the realization of how near he had come to killing Dare, steadied himself on the paint's heaving sides, Dare cried: "Sam, are you boys all right?"

"Sure, boss! They blowed a hole in the wall— that's all! We held 'em off till Cim got here. Did they git Madge?"

"No!" A fraction of Dare's suspense was eased. "They got——"

"Dare"—Mace's fingers closed like talons over his knees, his voice was hoarse with agony—"did he—— Man, tell me the truth—I can stand it! He got— Eloise!"

Eloise! Even then Dare had a wild impulse to laugh. Imagine even Red Madden kidnaping the teacher! But Mace loved her, as he himself loved——

"They got Allie!" he cried, spurring past.

Tearing through the court and around the house, he saw Corral de Terra's defenders fortified in the sycamores, facing a jagged hole in the wall. Their guns were silent, and a wild whoop of victory rent the air as he jerked rein beside his foreman.

"Don't stop, Cim!" he shouted. "We've got to git the gang! My Lobos are comin'! The fight ain't for the ranch! Red Madden——"

"He's gone!" Cim turned on Dare wild eyes, unearthly with the glare of the battle ligh. "He circled the wall, called off his dogs, an' went on!"

Dare pulled around. 'He's got Allie!" he cried desperately. "I'm after him, Cim!"

With a spring, Cim grabbed his bridle, held him, against Check's furious struggles as Dare spurred.

"You fool!" Cim cried, as he had on that night when they raised the old dust, but now in his great love for the boy. "They've gone to the ford! What could you do—fightin' a hundred men! What! We'll all go with you!"

Dare had just reason enough to see the wisdom in that. And he swung back, shouting for his men to drop everything here, let everything go, and follow to the ford.

As the cowboys and Cim's Lobos ran to horse, the Lobos Dare had outridden stormed into the court. Then ensued such a babble of high-pitched voices, as every man wanted to know what had been done, what was to do, that Dare—frantic, as each moment deepened the shadows, lessening his chances of rescuing Allie, and despairing of making himself understood—uttered the one cry that would pierce the chaos

"Ride, Lobos!"

He leaped the jagged ruins of the blasted wall, and they came after, across the plains, the lathered paint running stronger than ever, still leading them all. And Dare could see the outlaws, a dark blot, in advance. Straining his eyes on them, as they were bearing off his every hope of happiness, he saw them suddenly swing from their course, circling a butte, and saw the reason! For another dark mass loomed on the dusky horizon where they had been, and quickly neared them.

"The men at the ford! The cattle guard!" yelled Cim, firing six quick shots in the air—the Lobos' signal that friends were coming.

And the two galloping bands came together, pell-mell.

"Devlyn, take your men back!" Gid Perkins yelled. "There's a plot to blow up Corral de Terra! A rider came to our camp——"

"It was a trick!" Dare cried, having no time for explanations. "A trick to git you away from the ford—while they cross the sheep!"

The air was blue with execrations, as these men, too, swung in behind Dare.

And now he led them—Los Lobos cowmen!—in full force, a terrible force that nothing could stem. The ground rocked to their gallop, and on the still air beat the iron music of the range—the unforgetable, indescribably thrilling sound of hundreds of hoofs beating with a single purpose! And, in tuneful undertone, there rose the wild and inarticulate murmur of a hundred angry men, a fearful, pursuing voice that rang over the plains, and was carried through the mesquite and sage to the very crags of the lonely Nimbres. It was a voice that might have reached the frightened campers, making the slow trek out from Devil's Gorge on foot, that must surely rouse Lynne Jessimer from the deadly coma that claimed him still, as the buckboard wheeled slowly into the home court, that must have reached Swap Boone, just hearing from Madge's lips that his baby had purchased the safety of another girl at the cost of her own!

Up on the last prairie rise that sloped down to the ford, the iron music rang. Below, between the river forks, a triangle of land was stretched, tight as a drumhead, and as bare. Here, for weeks, the sheepmen had been intrenched. Here they had been when the cattle guard left. Across it, with a last spurt of speed, Red Madden's combined forces ran, and, reaching the boulder-strewn south bank of the Upper Rio, they flung down, prepared to make their stand, knowing that the cowmen must fight through. For here, too, natural barricades prevented attack from another quarter!

Dare, galloping over the bed of the lower stream, dry at this season of the year, and up on the denuded flats, saw that one of the riders kept on. Red Madden! For now the giant horse appeared, splashing through the shallow water, dragging his helpless captive after him. Fury would have mastered Dare, but for the roar that went up behind. The roar of maddened cowmen. For *the sheep were crossing!*

The gray mass of them bridged the river, overflowing on the north bank—cattle range since time out of the oldest Lobo's mind! Endless, the file of them floundering in the shallow ford after their leaders, endless the gray mass to come. Ruin, to the cattlemen; goading them almost beyond restraint.

Suddenly, with the crisis at hand, Dare realized the lives that depended on him. Everything was set for a wholesale slaughter—the bare thought of which filled him with shuddering horror. They must force the fight, end it quickly; for, in a quarter of an hour, it would be dark. By then, the sheep would be over, and, in the confusion and dark, Allie would be carried beyond all help to some secret hiding place

in the hills! She might even be held a hostage—her
life, the forfeit, if cowmen attempted to move the
sheep back!

Wildly his men surged about him, clamoring for
directions what to do. Some were borne past by the
very impetus of their fury and hate, and these were
met by a volley from the ambushed outlaws—a volley which, though it fell short, was grim warning that
death lurked in the next hundred yards Dare's impulse
was to charge straight through. But the futility of
that—on the open ground, and the criminal waste of
life it would entail, were all too apparent.

"Down, boys!" he ordered, yanking Check up.
"That's a game two can play at! Angle out for
them rocks! We'll make that nest too hot to hold
them!"

Leaping down, with drawn gun, he did not look
to see if they obeyed him. For his eyes were glued
on Red Madden, dragging the lead horse up the opposite bank, ruthlessly riding over sheep and herders.
But the men came, dodging from rock to rock, sway-
ing from side to side, eyes raking all around, after
their youthful leader, whose daring and reckless dis-
regard for life were lauded years after this night
became legend.

Monotonously, bullets whined among the rocks.
No target was visible, yet many a bullet found its
mark. Gloom dimmed the scene, even as the deafening bleats of thousands of frightened sheep muted
the sound of the battle waging. Every moment increased the cowmen's fury, as every moment increased by hundreds the number of sheep on their
range. Rock by rock, inexorably, slowly, the cowmen
fought to get within gunshot of the sheep and herders,

with the outlaws stubbornly contesting every foot of
the way.

Dare, thinking only of Allie—and the only one
who did, in the awful turmoil and din—fought in
blind frenzy. His gun smoked in his hand. His
sombrero was shot from his head. A flying
sliver of rock, bullet chipped from the boulder
he had just gained, cut his face like a razor, inflicting
a deep wound. But he worked through the rain of
lead unscathed. He did not know whether he killed
any one or not. He was never to know. In after
years he hoped he had not, as ardently as he now
prayed he might. For, in these age-long moments
of suspense he suffered all that Allie could suffer
if he failed to win her, and if Red Madden had
been double the fiend he was.

Old Cim, dodging to the rock behind which Dare
fought, found his eyes dim as he looked at him. All
that was boyish had passed out of his face forever. It was old—set in lines of pain and purpose.
Cim knew how bitterly Dare blamed himself for
this night's happenings, and how needlessly. What
had come to pass, would have come to pass, regard-
less of Dare Devlyn. Progress—the inevitable meas-
uring of hitherto unmeasured lands—had dealt the
cards for this grim game!

And Cim noted, too, how, to his own peril, the
boy's dark, yearning gaze kept darting through the
milling men and animals on the other bank. He did
not see what Dare never for a single moment lost
track of—Red Madden, sitting his horse in the quivering shadows of a knoll above the bank, coolly
watching to see how the battle turned, and ready, if
it went against him, to run with the prize which he

thought would "put him in clover" for the rest of his life. Visible, also, to Dare, was that prize, the frail girl pitifully drooping on the lead horse beside the outlaw. Cim's gaze missed Madden, as a sound drew his eyes back to that which piled fresh fuel on the fire of his wrath.

Over the open flats, heedless of the cowmen's guns, two horsemen lashed like mad, so stunning the cowmen by their courage, that not a gun was raised till they were out of range.

"Hardy!" Cim roared in Dare's ear. "Come to help his sheepmen! Oh, why didn't I drop him!"

Every cowman wondered that about himself. Their votes had elected Hardy, and they hated him for resigning the public's interests for his own—turning traitor to their trust. But they forgot it in their greater wonders at what they saw, for Hardy and the other rider, circling the milling sheep at a gallop, halted at the ford, where the herders and their employers were crowding the bawling hordes across.

The cowmen saw him spring down, rally the sheepmen around him, passionately addressing them—inciting them, they thought, for his words were lost. And they cursed him. But their curses died, in their astonishment, as the group scattered, and men cut through the crossing sheep.

"They're turnin' 'em back!" Old Cim was thunderstruck.

Dare wrenched his eyes from Red Madden, just as a man leaped up on the bank, waving high over his head something tied to a long stick—something that gleamed in the gloom, that set Dare's heart beating as though it were a banner of hope!

A resounding yell went up from the cowmen. "They've raised the white flag!"

"It's a trick!" Perkins made himself heard by sheer might of voice. "Why should they surrender? They've got things their own way! Boys, it's a——" Surprise struck him dumb.

For Hardy, closely backed by the others, was in the saddle, galloping for that outlaw-infested nest of rocks. He stopped. They heard him thunder some command. They heard its answer—oaths, shots! They saw a sheepman at Hardy's side topple, saw Hardy's gun fan on the rocks.

"By juniper," screamed a Lobo, "they're fightin' among themselves!"

All then was a bedlam, in which it was impossible to follow any man, or group of men. The sheepmen were charging for the rocks. The outlaws—again penned in between two fires—were frenzidly seeking their horses, with no order, and every man wholeheartedly for himself. And the Lobos, with guns ready for any emergency, dashed ahead.

"*Hold!*" cried Hardy, and they stopped, seeing no sheepman, but their sheriff—for a silver star flashed on his breast.

"Men," he cried, facing them with the cool nerve and magnetic force that had elected him, a sheepman, sheriff in a county where cowmen outvoted his faction two to one. "Men, drop this range question to-night! Our fight—the fight of every decent citizen—is with Red Madden's gang! Help me run these dynamitin', girl-stealin' cutthroats to earth! I ask you—every man of you—in the name of the law I'm here to uphold!"

And then they cheered him! A strange, yet natural reaction, for, as members of a family turn on the outsider who interferes in family quarrels, so did the Los Lobos cattlemen and sheepmen turn the full force of their hot hate on Madden's gang. Almost to a man, they joined the sheriff in the round-up. And the renegades ran for holes like rats. Some would find them across the border, some, six feet beneath the sod, and one, their cautious leader——

Dare Devlyn—whose eyes had never left him—saw Madden lash the big horse through the shadows, fighting with the lead horse, who, terrorized by all this turmoil, reared and bucked. He saw Madden, in desperation at being impeded by the frightened animal, jerk Allie free and, placing her before him, speed off upriver toward the brakes that gave way to the wild, secret places in the Nimbres. And before the shadows quite closed around the outlaw, a vivid, paint horse splashed through the ford, and up the bank in hot pursuit.

"Run, boy!" again Dare talked in Check's ear, man to man. "Run—if ever you ran!"

And he was not asking the impossible now!

CHAPTER XXIII

HAND TO HAND

NEVER had Check run before! So Dare thought exultantly, thrilling to his furious pace, beaten out on the wet, slick trail that followed the river into the hills. Check ran with every last reserve of lung, and heart, and limb, and, too, in that deceptive hour when trees, rocks, all things immutable seem to come to life and move and merge in grotesque measure so that the eye can to no single object cling. Yet, true as the needle to the pole, he relentlessly followed the black shadow that was Madden.

And the great black was worthy of Check's mettle. Red Madden's neck, which he prized so highly, frequently depended on his mount. Always, it was the best that could be had, and the black was the best he had ever had So he was confident of escaping the hornet's nest he had stirred up, and getting the girl away—over the border, maybe. Then from some safe place, he would start negotiations with Jim Grant, make that nabob kick through aplenty, for all the trouble he'd been to. He had tried to pull Cull Cole's chestnuts out of the fire, and Cole had shoved him in! But the sheepmen had done him a good turn—broken up the gang, so he would not have to split the ransom coin!

The half-fainting girl across his saddle shuddered at his laugh, and strained more intensely to catch

the sound of other hoofs beating with those of
Madden's mount. It was a sound that grew by seconds, until at last Madden heard, and spurred, and in
the next hard half mile began to doubt his ability to
shake off the Nemesis on his trail. And he cursed the
girl, whose added weight, slight as it was, was begin-
ning to tell on the black.

But Dare, riding as he had never ridden, bless-
ing Check each minute, had not a doubt on earth!
The instant he had splashed through the river ford
his anxious frenzy left him. A great calmness fell
upon his soul, an appalling confidence. He gloried in
the thought of coming to grips with Madden, that
he, alone, would rescue Allie. He did not know that
old Cim and the boys were behind, that, to them,
he was a moving shadow, pursued as desperately as
he was pursuing the outlaw. For Dare the night held
only Red Madden, himself, and the prize—a prize
incomparably dearer to him than all the gold the
renegade hoped to get from the man he thought was
Jim Grant.

So steadily did Check gain that now, as the trail
came out on the bank high over the dark water,
neither Dare nor Madden were shadows to each other,
but each assumed to the other the shape of an
enemy who blocked the path of life. So close were
they that Dare could see the white blur of Allie's
face turned toward him. His heart leaped with joy
that she knew help was coming, and it beat hard with
rage at the cruel torture she was undergoing—held
in that strained position, taking the full force of
every jar and jolt. He jerked his gun free in a fierce
thirst to use it, though he knew he dared not
shoot. It would be too dangerous to Allie to risk

a shot at Madden with both horses running at full
speed, too dangerous to drop the black, lest the
crash kill her. And he knew that Madden realized
his handicap!

Nearer Check gained, and nearer. He was so
near that, as Madden twisted in the saddle to look
back, Dare saw the snarl of fury on his face. With
every jump, Check gained, and the outlaw, shifting
Allie to his left arm, twisted again, raised his gun
over his shoulder and aimed. Red flame streaked the
night. Perilously close, a bullet whirred by Dare.

And the boy laughed! Recklessly, joyously, he
laughed, and spurred. Some twenty paces lay between them now. Again Madden turned with lifted
gun. At that short range, Dare knew he could not
miss. And he braced himself for the shock, still
uplifted by that conviction that all the guns on earth
could not prevent his saving the girl he loved. But,
in that nick of time, while the gun aimed over the
dark head on Madden's shoulder, Dare saw Allie
struggling, twisting, heard a fearful snarl of rage
and pain, and, over the thudding hoofbeats came
Allie's weak, triumphant cry:

"Quick, Dare, I bit him—good! He dropped his
gun!"

Murderously, Madden's fist rose over her——
That instant Check lunged beside the black, and Dare
leaped in a long arc from the saddle, his arms closing
about Madden's neck, bringing him and his helpless
captive crashing to the ground!

Least stunned by the impact, the cowboy, with cat-
like quickness, writhed from under, rolling Madden beneath, his arm clamping in a deadly hold about
his neck. But Madden was the more powerful of

the two, and an adept in the rough-and-tumble style
of combat—as a man must needs be to master half a
hundred of the toughest characters in the West.
With a heave of his body, he rolled the boy under.
But every ounce of sinewy strength in Dare's arm,
the whole life of him, was in that neck-breaking grip.
Nor could Madden shake it, and his furious struggles rolled them near that dangerous black brink.

Allie, thrown clear in the crash, lay just as she had
fallen. Still stunned, she had a very faint perception
of what went on. She knew vaguely that Dare and
Red Madden were in mortal combat near her. Yet
she could make no move. Her arms were bound,
and her muscles paralyzed from the terrible jolting
of that long ride from Devil's Gorge. Her brain was
benumbed by the horror of all she had thought and
seen since she had given herself into Red Madden's
hands. It was a tremendous effort merely to turn
her head and watch, with still more numbing horror, the fiercely struggling forms poised on the very
margin of the bank. She saw them heave again—
roll—vanish!

Desperately she tried to rise, but could not, and in
her frenzy, she rolled agonizingly over the stony
trail to the black bank. She might have rolled down,
too, but for the snag that caught her bonds and held
her. She could not free herself. And, thus pinioned,
she turned her face down, but saw nothing for the
brush grew upon the bank, and the night that lay
thick over all. But she could hear!

With ears grown mercilessly keen, she heard—over
the sad song of the water—a wild thrashing on the
gravelly beach down there, wheezing breaths, gasps,
groans. Dare was being killed by Madden—for she

heard the bandit curse! In her terror she cried to Dare, but he did not answer. She fought like a mad thing to her knees, lunged against the snag that held her until, wearing herself out, she fell on her back, to note with crazing anguish that the sounds were fewer, fainter—ceased altogether! She knew now that Dare was dead! She thought how he would lie there forever, and no one would know. She must tell Madden when he came up that she was not anything to steal—just a wagon tramp. Then he would kill her, and she could rest here with Dare.

Far from the black heights a coyote cried, and a shudder swept her. A star shone out in the sky above her, and she wondered how God could let the stars shine when Dare was dead. And piteously she moaned to it: "Star light—star bright—first star— I've seen—to-night——" She could not complete the rite—for Dare was gone, and there was nothing left to wish for.

Then with horror infinitely greater than any yet, she heard the victor coming! She could hear his heavy, halting steps groping up the bank, and she knew it was Red Madden—Dare never walked like that. She heard him breathe—coarse, horrid breaths, like those of a winded beast. Trembling, her blood freezing into ice, she waited, too horrified to hear the hoofs of horsemen pounding up.

For she saw it: A thing more frightful than all the ogres of her childish fancies, a thing of ghastly and inhuman shape! Huge and terrible it rose above the brushy bank, sagged to its knees, and rose again, stumbling toward her—— Her wild shrieks rent the night.

"Don't—girl!" it said, in a heavy, thick, unnatural

tone, as it threw off its inhuman guise. "I—brung him—up, Allie! See? He can't—hurt you—now!"

Vaguely, she knew that men were around them—Cim, Sam, Las Vegas, and——

"It's Red Madden!" she heard Dare say, as he keeled over. "Hobble him—if he needs it, boys!"

She had a faint impression of their examining Red Madden by the light of matches, deciding that he did not need it, and throwing him across his horse. Then she knew no more.

CHAPTER XXIV

SWIFTLY the Los Lobos Range fell back into the ways of peace. The great sheep horde was broken up into its original small bands, and each flock was returned to where it came from. The cattle herd was scattered again to the four corners of the range, and solitude possessed the Rio ford. Riderless horses were rounded up, and empty saddles stored, and fierce-eyed old-timers went back to their nooks and crannies, like old pumas tamed and docile.

For the guns laid down, figuratively, that night at the ford, were not taken up again. The force of fury had been expended in the outlaw hunt, and time had been given for sober, second thought. And, in the remorseful mood this thought engendered, both factions had yielded to the appeal of Sheriff Hardy and Prosecutor Holt to endeavor to settle by compromise, by law, what they had resolved to end by force.

The cow town of Sundown had witnessed a spectacle unique in its history—the convening of Los Lobos cattle and sheepmen for peaceful arbitration. Both sides, each having gained a new respect for the other, were anxious and willing to do what was right. But what could they do? The problem of range was vital and, apparently, as insoluble as before. Deferentially, they placed their problem before Dare

Devlyn, who had clinched the respect of all by his single-handed capture of Red Madden—now languishing behind bars, until in due time he should pay the penalty for his crimes. With amazing trust, they left to the youthful owner of Corral de Terra, who was most affected by it, what should be done with the North o' Rio range. And Dare had the courage to suggest the one course he thought right:

"Split it—fifty-fifty!"

And so, with ringing cheers, it had been done.

But this was merely the initial step toward cementing lasting peace. The sheepmen, not to be outdone in generosity, had volunteered through Cull Cole, their spokesman, to reduce their flocks, adopt a strict program of range conservation, and pasture higher in the Nimbres. And the harmonious meeting had reached a climax when the two old foes, Cull Cole and Gid Perkins, had buried the hatchet and shaken hands.

There would be more dissension. That is inevitable when the interests of two groups of men clash. But their good will and intent now, the tolerance of the younger generation—as evinced by Dare—augured well for future peace. The old dust was laid; storms of strife had cleared the air of old prejudice and passion; the sad and lonely spirit that had brooded over the Los Lobos was replaced by one of hope, and it slept as peacefully as on that day when Dare Devlyn had galloped into the range.

Three weeks had passed, and this was just another such day as that on which Lynne Jessimer—as Jim Grant—had arrived. Flowers splashed perfume and color in the old court of Corral de Terra. Birds spilled their liquid, golden notes. Sun gold flowed on the smiling face of El Capitan. It was hard to believe that tragedy had ever been there. And Dare sat on the gallery, thinking of all that had been, and all that was to be. He still bore the marks of his terrible conflict with Red Madden, but he had deeper wounds that would not heal. It was hard to him to believe in his own suffering.

In the midst of peace, his heart was at war. If, as some one has said, time is measured best by heart throbs. Dare had lived years since that night of storm. He felt old and, beyond words, lonely. And he looked ahead with dread to still more lonely times, for to-morrow his visitors were leaving in a body, as they had come.

He saw Sam and Las Vegas strike off over the sunburned hills to look after Corral de Terra's herd, and watched old Cim overseeing a crew of Mexicans that he had hired to repair the blasted wall. Moodily, Dare glanced at Mace, "shooting" Eloise in a graceful pose on the bench beneath the sycamores. Mace wasn't worth his salt these days. Dare understood that. A hombre wasn't much good when he was in love. But there was hope for Mace. With a pang of envy, he recalled their coming to him last night—Mace, proud as Punch, and Eloise, blushing like sixteen.

"Guess what, boss?" Mace had blurted sheepishly, for all his pride.

"No guess about it!" he'd told them. "It's weddin' bells for you!" And they had been so surprised to find he knew!

"No—I'll never teach again," Eloise had flut-

tered. "I wrote poppa that I was staying West
to be a cowboy's bride."

Well, Eloise wasn't a bad old girl, when you got
to know her. She'd make a good wife for Mace.
Everybody couldn't have Allie? *He* couldn't! And
that was killing him by inches. Jasper was the lucky
man. Oh, *they* hadn't announced it. But they didn't
need to! And Jasper was rich. He could give
Allie everything. She wouldn't care about an old
ranch house now. She'd have a Gascony château.
He'd found out what that was—a swell home, in a
foreign country. Well, she'd grace it—just as she
was. As if he'd ever have changed her the least
bit!

But Dare wished he could change the way she
felt about him! She had a smile for every one but
him. Even Madge now! Since that terrible night
the girls had been great friends, and Allie had avoided
him twice as much since that night. She'd thanked
him—yes. But, Lord——

"All by your lonesome, son?"

He looked up to see Lynne Jessimer.

"Yeah. Where is everybody?"

Lynne grinned. "Down to Swap's camp—to a
dude! Tradin' like sixty—for it's their last day."

As Kit had predicted, a bullet more had not killed
Lynne, had not even endangered him long. He was
a little pale, looked a little older, moved a little more
slowly—that was all.

"The last day," Dare echoed. "Gee, you can't
think how I hate to see 'em go, Lynne! All we've
been through together—the way everybody's acted—
Lynne, we're all such good ol' friends!"

"The best of friends must part," Lynne reminded him soberly.

He sat down beside the boy. For moments speech was smothered under the weight of their thoughts.

"Son," Lynne said presently, "may I have an old friend's privilege—get personal?"

"You sure may, Lynne!"

"Then—tell me, just how are you fixed? Financially, I mean."

Dare flushed, but he raised straightforward eyes.

"Bad fixed, Lynne. Up to my neck in debt. I thought I had all the money there was when I bought Corral de Terra. But my ten thousand went like July hail. It took most of it to rebuild the old place. Borrowed money to buy my herd—thinkin' I could make enough out of boarders to tide me along till the cows grew into money. But as a landlord, I'm a puncher! Been more outgo than income all the time. An', Lynne, when I think of interest, the next payment on the place——" Finally, then, remembering that he was speaking to the man he would owe that payment to, "But I'll make out—now I got my bearin's. I'm a cowman!"

"A cowman," Lynne repeated feelingly. "You're lucky you know it! Hold to it, son. I'm a cowman, too! But I forgot it—for thirty years. No—I *never* forgot it! It was in my blood. Night and day, I'd hear the range calling. How I'd long for it—a horse under me, and the world ahead, clash of horns and hoofs, smell of a camp fire, my blankets and the stars!"

"But you could have come back?" The boy wondered.

"Yes," Lynne owned, "I could have come back.

Any charges against me, or any of the Lobos, were outlawed long ago. It wasn't that. It was fear, I reckon. Fear of—memories. Besides, there wasn't anything to come back to—with Joe and Pete dead, and the old home wrecked. I made money, married, settled down, and tried to forget the past. I made no secret of it to my family. Madge has known since she was old enough to understand. When her mother died, I got restless—thought more of old days. I planned to come out and rebuild the ranch, but, before I got around to it, Kit wrote that he'd sold it. It was a shock, for I'd even forgotten that I'd listed it for sale, when I started out and needed money. But I had to come. And I've been happier here, than ever I—— Son, you don't want to sell, by any chance?"

Dare's distress was evident.

"No," Lynne said kindly, "I see you don't. Well, I don't blame you. But—boy, 'you need capital. How about selling me a half interest in Corral de Terra? Together, we could do things on a big scale. I wouldn't interfere!" He was pleading now. "My business will keep me East most of the time. I'm getting old, son. And it would be Heaven to come out here once a year, in the few years left me —come home—be a cowman!"

There was no refusing that appeal, nor did Dare want to. He did need capital. But best of all was the fact that he'd be partners with Lynne Jessimer —his hero still.

So they sat on and planned. That is, Lynne planned, and Dare assented to—he knew not what. For Allie and Madge had strolled into his line of vision, their arms about each other's waists, their heads close, in beautiful contrast, like shadow and sun. But it was Allie's dark beauty that held Dare's gaze. She looked like a little Queen of Sheba in that pink rig and slippers. Her dreams had all come true—without his help. Lynne had sent Madge with her to "pulverize" Mrs. Hutchins by buying out her store! Allie had balked like a little mule at taking money for what she had done—but she hadn't been able to refuse Lynne, any more than he had.

As the girls turned toward the gallery, Dare started, brightened, as Allie had that day at the river gate when she thought he was coming to her. And pain shot through Dare when, seeing him there, she ran back down the path—even as she had been pained that day when he went blindly on to Madge. But Dare did not know that Allie—any one—had ever felt like that.

He did not know that it was shame that made her shy—shame that she had shown her heart, she thought, to every one that night! Madge knew she loved Dare, so did Swap—she could tell it. And Dare must know it. That's why he wanted to be good to her—sorry for her! Oh, she'd go so far away that he couldn't see her—ever—ever pity her again!

All Dare knew was what she had told him—that she hated him! That's what he couldn't stand! Why, that night when they had carried her back, sick from shock, she wouldn't let them bring her to the house, but made them take her to the *Santa Maria*—where she'd lain for three days, tended just by Swap!

"Dare!" He looked up wearily, as Madge called to him.

"Come on out to the corral, Dare—I must say good-by to Check."

Slowly he went to where she waited, her sweet face almost as serious as his, and together they started. But once around the house, out of her father's sight, Madge stopped and laid both hands upon his arm.

"Dare"—there was pity in her blue eyes for him —"Allie's going East with us."

He stared at her like a man who has just heard his death sentence.

"She's going back for a year, Dare. Dad insists on it. He wants to give her every chance—for what she did for me."

Still, with stricken dark eyes, Dare stared.

"Dare"—Madge's tone was vibrant with earnestness—"why do you suppose Allie changed places with me up at Devil's Gorge?"

"Why?" he choked. "Because she's a thoroughbred —that's why! She didn't want you to——"

"No!" Madge smiled tremulously. "She's all you say, Dare. Nevertheless, she didn't do it for me— but for you!"

"*Me?*"—dazedly.

"Yes—you! She thought you cared for me. And she—— Gracious, but you men are dense! Dare, make it up with Allie, before she goes away!"

Madge sighed, as she watched him make tracks for the river gate. Intellect ruled her heart, and she had seen from the first how matters stood. Just the same, she had come very near loving Dare Devlyn.

On his way to Allie, Dare was happier than he had been in weeks. What Madge hinted wasn't true, of course, but just the thought made him loco! Allie wasn't going to marry Jasper anyways soon— maybe never—if she was going home with Madge for a year!

And he sang, as he went down the river trail:

> "I can hear the hungry coyote,
> As he sneaks up through the grass,
> In my li'le sod shanty on the——"

His song died as he came through the little clearing by the creek! There was the dingy tent, the *Santa Maria,* the old derelicts—augmented by the sorrel pony that had played such a part that fateful night. There were the dudes, squatted like natives around Swap's camp fire, and there, off to themselves under the cottonwoods, were Allie and Jasper Kade! Allie and Jasper, all excited—talking plans!

Strangely, it was Jasper, and not Allie, who held Dare's disappointed gaze. Not the bored pilgrim he'd first met, nor the savage he'd overtaken on the mountain trail, but Jasper in woolly chaps, flannel shirt, and ten-gallon hat, holding the reins of a horse that wore the Hondoo brand! Flashingly, Dare recalled that he hadn't seen much of Jasper this last week. He'd made himself mighty scarce around the ranch. Folks had remarked on it. What was he doing here with a Hondoo horse? What was he doing in that range get-up? What was he doing here, anyway, spoiling his chance to make up with Allie—who was going East—for a year!

"When you come back next summer," he heard

Jasper saying, "I'll have everything fixed! And I'll make a trip back about Christmas, Allie, and we'll——"

They both saw Dare standing there.

"Hullo, neighbor!" Jasper grinned, proud as Punch, proud as—Mace! "Behold a cowman! Congratulate me, man! I've bought the Hondoo Ranch, lock, stock, and barrel! This is the only place I ever saw where life was worth living—so, catch *me* leaving! We're going to be neighbors, Devlin!"

Dare mumbled something and got away. Blind, again! Tear blind, this time. He couldn't see Allie's gypsy eyes reflecting the pain that was in his own, or her hands going out to him!

Nobody saw Dare the rest of that day or night. Only Check knew how many miles were clicked off at furious pace, as he rode and rode under the white stars.

Empty saddles to haunt him always! Always to carry an empty heart!

Again, all Sundown was at the depot, this time, to meet the eastbound train and see Corral de Terra's guests depart. And they regaled the brief wait by jolly comments on the wagon loads of luggage— for, thanks to Swap, every dude was taking home three pieces of baggage for every one he'd brought. And those who knew told those who didn't know the big news—that Lynne Jessimer had bought in with Devlyn and was one of them again! Which is Lynne? Say, you must be a stranger here! That's him—talking to Kit Kress. And that's his daughter—over there, with Swap Boone's girl. You know the gritty kid who palmed herself off on Red Madden! You don't mean *that* little—— Sure, the one in the blue suit! Some swell, herself! Bet some rich hombre keeps her back East! What's wrong with Devlyn? He looks worse cut up than he did when Madden——

"Here comes the train!"

And Dare—crushed by adventure, doubting his ability to pick up the pieces, and staring his last at a big-eyed little figure in blue—was confounded by a babble of tongues.

"Remember, you've got a standing invitation——"

"Now be sure and write!"

"I've had the time of my life!"

"Bringing Mace back to Niagara Falls on your honeymoon, Eloise? No? Going to Devil's Gorge! Oh, you romantic folks!"

A near whistle. The departing guests overwhelmed Dare.

"Good-by, Dare!" The set look on his face brought tears to Madge's eyes. "I'll take good care of her."

Brokenly he answered "You're a good scout, Madge!"

"Good-by, pard!" That strong, manly clasp was Lynne's.

"Come East, Devlyn," said Ezra Biggers, in his plaid cap and plus-fours, lugging the golf bag that Swap hadn't been able to do him out of, "and I'll show you a game! Nothing like so strenuous as——"

"Good-by, Dare!" Tears in the voice of Mrs. Mills! "You've been wonderful to us! Yes, I'm certainly coming back——"

Good-by, the sensible three! Good-by! Good-by! Good-by!

The train whistled in, and Dare wanted to scream, then a little hand slipped into his, and a very small voice said: "So long, Dare!"

Thank God, she didn't say "Good-by"! What if he grabbed her, held her till the train went? Jasper was tugging at her arm. He'd see her Christmas! He'd have everything fixed when she came back! They'd be his neighbors!

"Adios, Allie!" was all Dare could say.

Then, as the train clanged and snorted in, came fleeting impressions: Allie in Swap's arms, and both in tears. Madge helping Allie up the steps, as though she was blind, too! All of them hurrying through the coach to the observation platform to wave last adieus. Swap, whimpering to him:

"She'll grow away from her ol' pop!"

"Not Allie—she's true-blue!" cried Dare.

"The *Santa Maria* won't look like much, after the swell places she'll be to! I ain't done right by Allie, Dare! I seen it—that night! My baby's got great stuff in her—looking how she swapped the cuckoo clock! I ain't fit to be her pop. That's why I'm lettin' her go. Lynne can do more for her than me! Me—I'm in her way——"

"Brace up, Swap!" If only he could keep a stiff upper lip himself till the train got away! "She'll see! Smile, if it kills you!"

"Good-by, baby!" waved the whiskery old trader, whose heart was breaking under his hickory shirt.

"Good-by, pop!" waved the regal little beauty he had fathered, standing up there with "high-toned folks," waiting to be whisked away!

And the train was moving, taking all the sunshine out of the world!

"Oh, Dare, I can't let her go! I'm losin' my——"

"Not *you*, Swap!" cried the boy in the anguish of his heart. "You'll have her back—in a year. Me—I've lost her forever!"

Swap was startled by an agony greater than his own. "What do you mean?" He stared.

"Why, she's goin' to marry Jasper, ain't she?"

A hand gripped Dare's shoulder and spun him about. It belonged to the new Hondoo owner.

"You're wrong, Devlyn!" Jasper put him right with a vengeance. "She won't have me on a bet! I've lost track of the times she's turned me down! I haven't a chance on earth. She made me see that last night—after you left camp! She's in love with some one—— Good grief, Devlyn, I hate to have such a dunce as you for a neighbor!"

The train was rapidly gathering momentum. The group at the rear—still wildly waving, trying hard to hold to faces that were fast becoming a featureless blur—were amazed to see a wild figure break away from the group, spring on the back of a flashy paint pony standing near, leap the platform, swerve on the track, and line out over the ties at breakneck pace. The train snorted disdain and put on speed. But all Check's marvelous speed was put in that short dash, and, foot by foot, he drew up, swung over the rail, strained alongside! And the wild-eyed cowboy on his back held out his arms, crying distractedly:

"Allie, *jump!*"

A little figure in blue climbed the railing, poised

there one split second, and leaped into arms that closed like steel around her! And as Check's momentum carried them on, the deliriously happy boy sobbed: "Allie! Allie! Allie!"

As happily she cried: "I'd have jumped off by myself in another minute, Dare!"

"I couldn't let you go! You've got to stay—give class to the old house—be my li'le housekeeper—— No—*wife!*"

Faint cheers came from the fast-receding train.

THE END.

Cherry Wilson enjoyed a successful career as a Western writer for twenty years. She produced over two hundred short stories and short novels, numerous serials, five hardcover books, and six motion pictures were based on her fiction. Readers of *Western Story Magazine*, the highest paying of the Street & Smith publications where Wilson was a regular contributor, held her short stories in high regard. Wilson moved from Pennsylvania with her parents to the Pacific Northwest when she was sixteen. She led a nomadic life for many years and turned to writing fiction when her husband fell ill. The first short story she sent to *Western Story Magazine* was accepted, and this began a long-standing professional relationship. If thematically Wilson's Western fiction is similar to that of B.M. Bower, stylistically her stories are less episodic and, as her experience grew, exhibit a greater maturity of sensibility. Her early work, especially, parallels Bower rather closely in that she developed a series of interconnected tales about a group of ranchhands. There is also a similar emphasis on male bonding and comedic scenes. Wilson stressed human relationships in preference to gun play and action. In fact, some of her best work can be found in those stories that deal with relationships between youngsters and men, as in her novel, *Stormy* (1929), and short stories such as 'Ghost Town Gold' which has been collected in *The Morrow Treasury of Great Western Short Stories* (1997). Three of Wilson's novels served as the basis for the Buck Jones production unit at Universal Pictures in the 1930s. *Empty Saddles* (1929) and *Thunder Brakes* (1929), book publications of serials first appearing in *Western Story Magazine*, are among her finest Western novels.